TALES FROM THE DARK COAST

Michael J.P. Whitmer

2022, TWB Press
www.twbpress.com

Tales from the Dark Coast
Copyright © 2022 by Michael J.P. Whitmer

Edited by Terry Wright

Cover Art by Terry Wright

ISBN: 978-1-959768-02-9

Table of Contents

Original cover art by Michael J.P. Whitmer

All the Toppings

The Dark Coast had a way of exhuming its sordid past. Before the French armada reached the coast and sailed up the St. John's river to claim territory for their king, the Timucua natives of this land lived in peace with their gods. In their temple, they'd built a stone altar in which sacred fires burned eternally for Ela, the Sun God. They believed the very breath of Ela existed in the flames, and at times, during certain special ceremonies, Ela demanded the sacrifice of a firstborn son. The French were not impressed with such savagery, conquered the Timucuans, enslaved them, and forced them to abandon their temple to the shifting sands of the dunes along the coast. As time passed, the Spanish defeated the French, and the English defeated the Spanish, and the revolutionaries defeated the British and founded America. All the while, the fires of Ela burned eternally under the dunes.

Then came Stephen Esposito to the site, a pizza magnet from up north where his family's empire had crumbled under the greed and mismanagement of his older brother, Anthony. It was here along the coast that Esposito would start anew, and he set about to dig the foundation for his new pizzeria. He scrutinized every move the construction team made as they leveled the dunes with a bulldozer.

Across First Street, a few beachgoers lined up for brunch at the Aqua Lounge, his only competition for the thousands of tourists and retirees who would soon occupy the high-rise apartments and resorts under construction in the area.

"Sir Esposito." The foreman tapped his shoulder. "You going to want to see what we found while digging."

Esposito's mind raced with visions of gold and jewels, for he had heard the legends of pirates that had pilfered shipping all up and down the coast. Could the team have found buried treasure? He climbed the mound of sand and stared into the pit the bulldozer had dug, its blade jammed against a solid stone structure. "What is it?" he asked the foreman.

"Hot. Very hot."

There was evidence of scorched logs and human bones scattered about. He instantly knew the ramifications of such a find. The government would shut down the construction and send in anthropologists and scientists to dig up and study the ancient relics. His pizzeria dreams would be dashed. Then again... "Hot you say?" He scrambled down the mound to see for himself.

Indeed, the find was hot enough to bake pizzas in, but what fueled such an oven? It appeared to be two-tiered, the top opening much narrower than the bottom, the base of which was higher than the water table, as the ground was dry. He envisioned an upper and lower level to his pizzeria... "Stop digging. We'll build around it." No one need know what they had found.

An elderly man clothed in moss and animal hide, and entirely tattooed, appeared from behind the hot stone structure. "Bury it," he said in a gravelly voice.

Esposito stepped back, alarmed. "Who are you?"

"They call me Ethore, the Timucuan shaman, exiled by the French, as this site was the sacred temple of Ela, our Sun God, which was my place to protect. This hallowed ground was desecrated by Menéndez's soldiers in the Massacre of Matanzas Inlet. The entity that lives in this altar must not be allowed to escape. See for yourself the death and destruction."

Around Esposito, the pit transformed into a scene from the past. Spanish soldiers with swords drawn stormed the beaches and cleaved off the heads of French settlers and their Timucuan captives then heaved their headless bodies into the temple's fiery altar that had been restored to its former splendor, right before his eyes.

"Ela will demand of you more of the same," Ethore proclaimed. "Leave this place before you live to regret it."

"Don't listen to him," a hollow voice said in Esposito's mind. *"We can be partners. I will restore the riches your brother denied you. All I require is the sustenance of souls."*

Today, built around the altar to Ela, stands the pizzeria known as All the Toppings, and they do a whopping business with their all-meats delight, though there are some folks who don't appreciate a hot, greasy pie.

Brodie, forcing calm, skidded his old Ford truck to a stop in All the Toppings' empty parking lot. The patrons had cleared out since he had picked up his pizza order earlier that night. His sister, Lonnie, had chastised him for not checking the contents of the box before driving off, but it was the last pizza of the day, and as he was walking out, the rabid vibes of those who'd stood in line waiting for a pie made him exceedingly uneasy. "If looks could kill," he told her, "I was a walking dead man."

"Take it back."

He shut off the engine and heard the annoying thump of hard rock music from the Aqua Lounge across the street. He wished it had been brunch-time and he had ordered one of their sushi-veggie burritos instead of a cheese-only pizza from this hole in the wall pizzeria. However, he'd trusted the online reviews: All the Toppings was rated a whopping five stars as the best spot along the Dark Coast strip for a slice of deliciousness. That was about to change. After tonight, if management didn't exchange this fat-oozing pizza for a cheese-only, he'd rip them a new asshole with a scathing review on Yelp dot com.

He bailed out of his truck, grabbed the soggy pizza box from the back bed, and stormed to the front door, leaving a drip-trail of grease on the asphalt. Despite the unlit neon OPEN sign in the window, he tested the door. Locked. A small sign read: Deliveries Only, with an arrow pointing to a doorbell button, which he pressed with urgency. A buzzing noise filled the inside of the dark establishment.

No one responded.

He pounded on the door with his fist. "I know you're in there."

A pale, bald man emerged from the darkness and opened the glass door a crack. "Get the hell out of here. We're closed," he hissed, and before Brodie could form a thought to reply, the black-eyed man closed the door and slithered back into the shadows.

"My name is Brodie. I spoke to Edgar over the phone about a wrong pizza you gave me." Brodie kicked the door with his hiking boot. "I ordered cheese only." He held up the dripping box and lifted the lid to reveal a fully intact all-meats pie. "I can't eat this shit."

The man reappeared behind the glass. "Like I said on the phone, there is only one pie on our menu. We're famous for our all-meat toppings."

"It's disgusting."

Edgar reopened the door, extended a well-manicured hand into the box, and peeled out a slice of pizza. After taking a huge bite and tossing it back, "Cold, but it tastes perfectly delicious," he mumbled, chewing.

"That's it. I want to speak to the owner, or I'm really ripping this backwoods shithole apart when I give it my review on Yelp." Brodie shoved the box into Edgar's hands. "And I want my money back."

As Edgar took hold of the box, the sleeves of his chef's coat rose up his arms, exposing clusters of tattoos that couldn't be distinguish from burns and blemishes. He flashed Brodie a slanted leer. "Sure. Follow me. I'll get your refund and fetch Mr. Esposito."

Brodie allowed Edgar to lead him through the front lobby where several chairs sat on either side of decorative shrubbery in the corner. The glow from a flickering streetlamp and a quarter moon strained through the storefront's tinted glass. An emergency exit sign at the other end of the dining room lit the way across the restaurant. As he entered the kitchen, Edgar flipped the light switch. Along the far wall and still radiating heat, stood a large, eerily antique brick oven.

Edgar stopped at a stainless-steel table where he set down the pizza box next to an array of knives, and then slipped into a vinyl dishwashing apron to cover his chef's attire.

Brodie seethed with impatience. "Quit stalling and give me my money."

Edgar picked up a chopping knife, spun around, and wielded the blade across Brodie's throat with a quick well-rehearsed swipe. A red mist spewed from the gash and sprayed Edgar's face.

Brodie tried to scream but gurgled and choked on blood. He staggered, fell forward, and in a panic, groped at Edgar. Instead of a helping hand, Edgar began a barrage of blade thrusts into Brodie's chest. He couldn't breathe. He couldn't see, the kitchen distorted as Edgar dragged him to the oven. His brain got caught in a loop. *Cheese only. That's all I wanted. Cheese only...*

Edgar shoved Brodie's twitching body into the fiery opening. The heat seared his eyeballs, set his hair ablaze, then mercifully, as he plummeted into a deep dark hole, everything went blank.

\#

Lonnie sat in the lobby of All the Toppings with her legs crossed, awaiting an interview for a job as a delivery driver. She fought a nervous tremble in her hands. The local authorities had dismissed her brother's disappearance as just another hiker from the Oldport Park campgrounds. With the swamplands and the long stretch of highway leading to the theme parks, missing out-of-town motorists and backpackers were not uncommon. Without a body, there wasn't enough probable cause to warrant a full investigation. "He'll turn up," they'd told her, so she had to take matters into her own hands.

Brodie was the only family she had left. This pizzeria was the last place he'd gone. He came here because of her. She'd told him to take the pizza back. She wouldn't eat all that grease. And he never returned. Something had gone terribly wrong.

She'd dreamed Brodie was standing in front of All the Toppings, holding the pizza box. Instead of grease, the to-go box dripped blood. The last time she had a dream about him, he'd gotten lost during one of his Cub Scout camping trips, acting like an Eagle scout when he was just a Cub. He was stuck in a cave. The search party was amazed when she led them to him. How was that possible, she'd asked her parents. They told her it was a special connection between twins.

Right about now, she regretted accepting the scholarship to Dark Pointe Marine Institute. Brodie, her twin brother, had warned her about the Dark Coast, its dark history, and the mysterious goings-on in the region. From pirates to shamans to cults, the slaughter of natives, and the disappearances of women and children, this was no place to call home. He had wanted to travel into the nation's wild, backpack and hike the Rocky Mountains on long-forgotten pioneer trails, and swim in the hot springs that burbled up around ancient volcanos. Brodie was no coward, but the Dark Coast scared the hell out of him.

However, she wanted to become a marine researcher, explore the mysteries of the sea, and maybe find a cure for cancer or other diseases, cures that would have prevented their parents' early deaths. Her goals were admirable, he'd thought, and agreed to postpone his adventures until she was established in her career. Then he'd set off to write his book and become the Henry David Thoreau of their time.

It couldn't be for that reason he'd disappeared. He would have told me first.

No. It was all about a cheese-only pizza.

She clutched her handbag and felt the steel form of the 9mm gun she'd only fired once, on the practice range. Still, it offered some assurance of protection, but from what she didn't know. From what her brother had said, the townsfolk swore by the pizzeria and tried to eat a slice at least once a day. However, the store's hours of operation were sporadic, claiming they were out of stock on toppings, sometimes closing early, or for weeks on end, but never during the summer months and holidays.

The chef rounded the corner and headed toward the back of the restaurant where stairs led up to Esposito's office. Regular customers had gathered outside the entrance, pressing their hungry faces on the glass, though the sign on the door read: *Out of stock.* She wondered if that were true or not, so when the chef was out of sight up the stairs, she darted from the lobby and headed for the kitchen. In the back of her mind, she had her looking-for-the-bathroom excuse ready in case she got caught roaming around.

In the kitchen, the weathered stone oven caught her attention. Soot blackened the rough rocks that surrounded an open maw, and flames danced around black racks, possibly made of solid slate. She imagined this same oven baking handmade clay bowls and water vases used by the ancient tribes who'd lived along this coast. Today, however, the oven exuded a tantalizing aroma of melting cheese, spiced sauce, and ground meat pies baking in the open chamber. Even her vegetarian palate responded wantonly to this delightful concoction of flavors on the rise.

She examined the smooth surface of a stainless steel table, polished clean, and an assortment of prep knives neatly laid out. She saw no evidence of toppings in stock, no cheese, no mushrooms, no pepperoni, but she knew the chef would return soon to attend the baking pies, so she didn't dally looking further. Near the back wall stood a dishwashing machine, and above it hung an old wooden meat-smashing mallet, an obvious decoration. There was nothing in sight that would indicate Brodie was ever here, just as his truck wasn't in the parking lot either.

"Lonnie."

A draft from the back of the kitchen carried the whisper of her name, which raised the hairs on the back of her neck.

"Lonnie."

"Brodie. Brodie. Is that you?" She rushed past the dishwashing machine to a staircase that led beneath the restaurant, its depths lying in shadow.

"Lonnie."

She heard her name rise up from the darkness and moved to look down the dark stairwell. "Brodie? Are you down there?"

"Lonnie? What are you doing in here?"

She whirled around, clutching her handbag, and saw the chef standing by the oven. He looked mad enough to spit nails. "Oh...sorry...I'm looking for the bathroom."

"You won't find it down there. Restrooms are by the rear exit under the staircase. Mr. Esposito is ready to see you now."

#

Lonnie ascended the steps, pretending the chef watching her by the restroom doors wasn't weird. He'd made sure she'd taken a direct route to the staircase. At the top, a hallway was lined with shelves stocked with canned tomato sauce, bottled water, and sacks of flour. She came to a door marked OFFICE, left ajar. "Mr. Esposito?"

"Come in," he shouted.

She stepped inside. "I'm here for the driver's job."

"Hello, Lonnie. My name is Stephen Esposito." He stood and extended a hand to her. "I've got your resumé right here."

She shook his beefy hand then seated herself in a chair in front of his desk. Esposito looked like a typical middle-aged man, slightly bent at the shoulders and sporting a big belly. His mostly dark hair was well trimmed and gelled over, making the streaks of gray shimmer. He wore a Zorro-sharp mustache, and his black polo shirt, embroidered with an *All the Toppings* logo, was tucked into faded blue jeans. He sat at his keyboard and typed something that coaxed a site to appear on his monitor.

As he studied it, she glanced past him at a wall of wine racks. An arm's reach away from his chair stood a double-barreled shotgun propped against a small combination safe. Alongside the desk, a six-segmented screen displayed views of the front parking lot, front door and lobby, dining room, the kitchen where the chef was boxing pizzas fresh from the oven, the alley behind the restaurant where a refrigerated produce truck was parked near a dumpster, and a dungeon of a basement, dark but for the flicker of furnace flames that illuminated chains hanging from the rafters.

The desk was cluttered with paperwork. Framed photos on the wall were mostly of groups of men in aprons or suits, posing in different restaurants. She could make out a younger Esposito in many of them. One picture was a portrait of a man dressed in depression-era clothes and a dapper fedora. "Who's that gentleman?"

Esposito followed her line of sight. "That's my grandfather. He taught me everything I know about pizzas." He closed out the internet site. "Your background check is clean." Then he picked up her resumé from the desktop clutter and read aloud. "So you go to the Marine Institute... a major in microbiology... You last worked at the campus café..."

The phone rang. He glanced at the caller ID and frowned. With a press of a button, he silenced the phone. "Do you have reliable transportation?"

"I do, yes, sir." She didn't want to admit her old mini-van was falling apart.

"That's important. As the owner, I wear many hats here, and handling all the deliveries is becoming too much for me. So you'll come in three times a week. The job pays minimum wage plus tips. Edgar, my chef, will have the orders ready for you—"

Ring.

The telephone interrupted him again. More forcibly this time, he mashed the button, and the ringing ceased.

"Sorry about that. So do you have any questions?"

She summoned the prepared words for the interview, but nerves delayed her speech. She gripped her handbag and could feel the pistol inside. "Do you deliver outside the swamp?"

"We don't. The deliveries are catering orders only...mostly to the town hall, hospital, and sheriff's office."

Lonnie nodded. "After summer, I'd have to resign for school. Will that be a problem?"

"Of course not. I'm flexible. A good education is important—"

The phone cut Esposito's words short, but he let it ring.

"So, when can I start?"

A brief chuckle and smile held the angered look from surfacing again. "Tomorrow. You have an order of ten pies to the daycare center."

She stood to leave. "You need to take that call."

"Yes, Of course, Lonnie. Excuse me."

At the door, he stopped her. "Oh. One more thing. Edgar may wear a permanently pissed off expression but he'll warm up to you, in time."

"I can't wait." She shut the door but lingered to listen in as Esposito picked up the call.

"I told you to stop calling. No, don't come over here."

Edgar, the chef, was standing at the end of the hall near the stairs, glaring at her. Fighting panic, she waved meekly.

He grabbed two large cans of tomato sauce then turned to go down the steps.

"I got the job."

"Good for you," he said over his shoulder, not a smile or word of congratulations.

For all she knew, he was the last person to see Brodie, but he definitely wasn't happy she'd discovered the stairs to the basement. She had to get down there to see if Brodie had whispered her name. He could be tied up as punishment for complaining about a pizza, but more likely she was losing her mind. Brodie might turn up with a new girlfriend tomorrow, and this job might earn Lonnie enough money to fix her van. Then again, desperate people grasped any ray of hope they could imagine.

#

Lonnie put the old mini-van into park and turned off the engine to kill the rattling noise. The parking lot was packed for being this near to closing time. Her first delivery was a success. She had received a tip of twenty dollars and now only needed to drop off the credit card receipt and collect her money.

The sign on the front door read: *Out-of-Stock for Today.*

Inside, patrons were mostly tank-top and flip-flop clad swamp folk faithful, stuffing the last bites of their slices into their eager mouths. Some guests cashed out with Edgar while he patrolled the dining room with a dish cart and cleared dirty tables. In one booth sat a father, mother, and their teenage son and daughter, all wearing theme park hats with animal ears. The family gorged on the local fare, leaving not even the crusts.

Edgar made eye contact with Lonnie and motioned her toward the kitchen.

The chatter and munching from the dining room seemed distant in the empty kitchen. She noticed one pizza baking in the oven...and a murmuring sound. She drew nearer and thought the murmur was actually the whispers of her name. Terror gripped her by the throat. She dared to get as close to the oven as the heat would allow.

"Lonnie," belched from the glowing maw.

A rush of heat and steam blasted her in the face, sending her backwards. "What the...?"

Edgar laughed. "You get too close you get burned." He was standing at the entrance to the kitchen. "The guests are almost gone." He moved past her to grab a wooden peel near the oven then shoveled the pizza out and slid it onto the stainless steel cutting table. "Want some?" he asked as he divided the pie eight ways with a rocking knife. "It's the last pizza until Mr. Esposito returns with more toppings." He didn't hesitate to scoop up a steaming slice and chomp into it with no regard for temperature or searing his tongue.

Lonnie studied the pizza. Ground chucks of meat were dripping grease into a blend of cheeses. The toppings sat in a secret red sauce that oozed over the edges of a golden crust. Her vegetarian conviction kept her from accepting his offer. "No thanks. I don't eat meat."

Edgar gave her a titled look and continued to gnaw. "You remind me of someone." He took another bite.

Staring at him, she thought he might have meant Brodie, as her twin brother looked a lot like her...or vise versa, but she forced herself to remain quiet and not suggest it might have been his face Edgar had found similar to hers. She didn't know him well enough to press for answers, how he might react if he knew she was onto him, that she knew this was the last place Brodie had gone to that night.

"What are you lookin' at?" he asked while chewing.

Edgar's scowl jerked her from her musings.

"Oh. Sorry...just wondering if you need any help cleaning up out there."

"And pay you? Nice try. I'll handle it. You got the delivery receipt?"

"Oh, yeah." She handed him the charge slip. "You owe me twenty bucks."

"Damn, twenty bucks for one delivery. Good going. I need your job."

She grinned at him. "Maybe it's time to ask Mr. Esposito for a raise."

"Fat chance." He finished off the slice and wiped his hands on his apron before pulling out a zippered envelope filled with cash. "I'll have another order for you tomorrow...same time," he said as he paid her.

"Alright." She put the twenty-dollar bill in her purse, next to the gun, then turned to exit the kitchen. Overhead and cornered where the ceiling and the wall joined, she noticed a camera. The sight made her think of the security screen in Esposito's office and how there could be footage from the night her brother was here. She looked back at the empty oven, recalled the murmur of her name, now silent, and thought it must've been the pizza's meaty gasses sizzling and hissing in the heat.

#

A midnight-blue MX-5 convertible sped into All the Toppings' parking lot, executed a 180 degree skid, and screeched to a halt backwards in a parking spot. From the passenger side, a blonde, fifty-something-year-old trying to look twenty-something, her face caked with makeup, squealed in excitement at the reckless maneuver. Her dress was panty-shot short and matched the color of the car. A silver-haired man, older than the woman, hopped out of the driver side. He wore a black suit, a silk tie, a gold necklace. and sported a spray-on tan. Shades, cologne, and chewing gum, he hoped would hide his earlier overindulgence in wine, blow, and tobacco. "Wait here, Haley. I shouldn't be long."

She huffed. "I want to come, please."

"It's business, babe. Just sit tight and pretty."

She sat there, pouting.

Edgar watched from the window. "He's here," he called to Esposito who sat in one of the lobby chairs, seemingly deep in thought.

Esposito stood and brushed invisible

lint from his black polo shirt. "Go to the basement. Be ready. We need to make this as quick as possible before Lonnie gets back. Plus, I have a shipment to pick up."

Edgar nodded and, with a smirk, he hustled off toward the kitchen stairway, thinking of what his value was to this operation and what his compensation should be for going above and beyond his paygrade.

Esposito opened the door before his brother could ring the bell. "Anthony."

"Little bro, you're lookin' good." He hugged Stephen and kissed his cheek.

"I told you not to come," Stephen said bluntly while pushing his older brother away. "You need to get the hell out of here."

"You're not going to chase family away from your door. Show some respect. It's important."

Stephen looked past him to wave at the last patron driving out of the lot with the last pizza of the day. All the Toppings was all out of toppings. He saw the woman in the sports car, lumping on more makeup to hide the wear and tear of being ridden too hard and put away wet too many times. The fact that his brother hadn't come alone complicated matters. He locked eyes with Anthony. "Alright, come in and state your piece. Does your girlfriend want to wait inside?"

"No. She'll be fine. She has a mirror to keep her company."

#

Up in Stephen Esposito's office, he sat at his desk and sipped his pinot noir while watching his brother down the last of his second glass before pouring a third. Family photos on the wall showed Anthony posed in many of them, arm-in-arm with his brother, the good old days when he wasn't the family leach.

"What do you think?" Anthony

rambled on from a chair in front of the desk. "You and me. All I need is a few months, and I can get you the seed money." He wanted his hands in the cookie jar again but hadn't said much more than, "It's a sure thing." He'd said it for the tenth time.

Stephen was keeping count. "Anthony, you had a sure thing...we had a sure thing, Mr. Eazzy Pizzas, the family business. Remember that? You said you saw a bigger picture. I told you not to sell, told you it was not what grandpa or dad would have wanted. You sold out anyway. Now that you've pissed all your money away, you've come to me for more. You haven't learned a goddamned thing."

"I didn't come here to get lectured by my kid brother. Fork up the cash, and let's get back to the way things were in the good old days."

"Sorry, bro. I'm a little strapped right now."

"Bullshit." Anthony shot up from his chair, knocking it over. "I know you have the funds, Stephen."

"What the hell makes you think that?"

"I saw your online accounts, your six-figure balances."

"You snake." Stephen stood nose-to-nose with his brother. "How could you possibly know that?"

"You always use the same password... A small joint like this, open a handful of years, in the middle of nowhere... I want to know how you made that much dough. If the franchisees find out you're getting rich on recipes that don't belong to our family no more, they'll sue our asses."

"I'm not using family recipes, besides, this is a one-horse pony show. There are no franchisees."

"Whatever it is, legit or not, I want in." Spittle flying from his mouth, Anthony gripped Stephen's shirt desperately. "I'm family, you hear."

"Alright. Follow me to the basement." Stephen unfolded his brother's hands from his shirt. "I'll show you the secret to my success."

Stephen led him downstairs, through the kitchen, and stopped at the edge of the steps to the basement. Anthony peered down into the darkness. "Seems like an odd place to have stairs. Dangerous for workers..." His words stalled as he heard the thumping of nightclub music below.

"What is it? What do you sense?" Stephen determined his brother was hearing the malevolent voice that dwelled in the furnace.

Tony tuned in closer. He could hear women's laughter and smell their perfume swirling with the smoke of his favorite cigar. "You got a speakeasy down there?" he asked, taking the first step down.

Esposito reached for the mallet hanging over the dishwashing machine. He swung and connected with the back of his brother's head. With a grunt from the blow, Anthony tumbled down the stairs.

He awoke with blurry sight and his head aching. There was a sharp pain in his back where a meat hook pierced his flesh. He realized he was suspended above the floor, dangling on a chain attached to the ceiling. He cried out in agony.

His vision came into focus to see his clothes and Haley's blue dress draped over a wooden...altar?...splattered with blood. His cry of agony morphed into a scream that the dirt walls absorbed.

"Haley."

"I don't think she can hear you, buddy." As evidence, Edgar picked up an ear from a mound of dismembered body parts. He dropped the ear on a metal tray attached to a conveyer that stretched to the mouth of a primeval oven. The brick and iron structure looked to be the first design of a colonial crematorium or forge and rose through the ceiling and took up the entire back wall. The tray of macabre body parts moved into the fire for a good cooking. "When we say all the toppings, we mean all the toppings." Edgar laughed.

"Enough," Esposito shouted from the shadows and stepped toward Anthony with the meat-tenderizer mallet in his hand.

"Stephen. Help me."

A voice from the flames of the furnace whispered in Stephen's ear. *"Anthony would do worse to you for less of a gain. He's always spited you, never loved you, and he strived against your happiness. End him."*

"You never loved me." Esposito raised the mallet. "I told you not to come here looking for handouts."

"No," he cried. "I'm sorry."

The first swing to his brother's forehead silenced him; the second hammering split his skull open. His third swipe made sure Anthony Esposito would be dead before going under Edgar's knives and into the fire. He dropped the mallet. "Edgar, handle the butchery before Lonnie gets back from her delivery. I'll dispose of the vehicle and then pick up the shipment." Esposito stared for a fleeting moment at his brother's limp body swaying on the hook. "See what your mooching got you, bro? You should have stayed away." He trudged up the stairs, past the oven that would soon be baking as many pies as the racks could hold.

At the front door, he flipped over the *Out of Stock* sign and switched on the OPEN neon sign. All the Toppings was back in business.

#

After leaving her broken-down van on the side of the road, Lonnie had to walk the remainder of the way to All the Toppings. The damn engine rattle had turned to a knock just before it quit. A growing puddle of oil underneath told her she'd probably lose this job before she found her brother.

She passed by Tetris Storage where a gang of punks were hanging around the wrought iron gate and lounging on the units' rooftops. Hard Rock music blasted from a boombox, and one guy was shooting rocks at the Tetris sign with a slingshot. None of them looked old enough to drive so she didn't bother asking for a ride.

Finally back at the pizzeria: "Edgar?" she called into the dark warm dining room. The restaurant felt hotter than usual. "Hello?" She entered the kitchen. The heat was hottest in here and emanated from the oven where unattended pizzas were burnt to the color of charcoal.

She climbed the stairs to Esposito's office. "Mr. Esposito?" She neared the partly open door to his office and saw the room was empty, which gave her an idea. *This is my chance to access the security cameras.* She figured the video footage would be stored on the computer on the desk.

Just looking for a tow-truck, she thought while sitting down in Esposito's chair. *Checking my school email.* She continued going over what to say if she were discovered.

The computer beeped and requested a password. She typed out All the Toppings as one word, but it failed. She looked around the room for a clue. Her glance fell on the label of an empty wine bottle next to the keyboard. Pinot noir failed. Her gaze raced over the office's furnishings again and finding the plaque below the portrait of Esposito's grandfather, she typed in Tommy Esposito, feeling confident as the machine took longer to process. The monitor went black. She was locked out and bowed her head in defeat.

The security monitor clicked on, and she looked up to see the screen flicker to life. A menu popped up on the computer monitor, dates and times, so she clicked on the night Brodie had brought back the pizza. The time stamp in the corner of the frame confirmed the date and time, and suddenly she saw Brodie's truck pull into the parking lot. On the next screen section, Edgar guided Brodie through the dining room, and then the kitchen camera revealed Edgar slashing Brodie's throat and tossing him into the oven.

Shock hit her like a sledgehammer, pooling her eyes with tears and stealing her next breath. She gasped. "No, Brodie." That goddamned Edgar. She had to make a copy of the video to take to the police. Hands shaking, she looked around the cluttered desk for a flash drive, in the desk drawers. Nothing. She picked up the desk phone to call the cops. No dial tone.

The computer beeped.

When she looked back to the security monitor, the time and date stamp had changed to real time, and the screen section of the basement view revealed a live feed of Edgar on his knees, nude, before the face of the ancient oven. His collection of chef knives were displayed on the floor around him. Hands clasped, he was clearly praying.

Before she could wonder any further, Esposito showed up on the alley screen, pushing a cart of black bags from the refrigerated truck. He stopped at the back door. His face warped into something fierce, as if he'd sensed treachery afoot in his business. Her heart and mind erupted with panic as she sought a place to hide. She ducked under the desk just as the door pushed open. Holding her breath, she reached into her purse to grip the gun. Esposito grabbed the shotgun and marched back out of the room. She peeked out from under the desk. The coast was clear. She stood to watch Esposito on the security screen stalk through the kitchen and down into the basement.

In the corner of the basement, Lonnie spotted Brodie balled in the corner, hugging himself. Getting as close to the monitor as she could, she couldn't believe her eyes. The image of her brother looked up from his knees to the camera as if looking straight at her.

Brodie's alive.

#

"My knives, I pledge... My life, I pledge to you," Edgar chanted, still kneeling on the floor. "I will serve you, my lord of darkness."

The sound of Esposito loading shells into the shotgun behind Edgar caused him to freeze.

"Edgar? What do you think you're doing?"

"I am under appreciated and under paid." He stood to face his boss, unashamed to be naked in front of him. "Without me, your pizza toppings would be the usual fare of lame meats and wilted veggies. I'm tired of being your lacky. I'm the backbone of this restaurant, so I'm taking over." His voice sounded as possessed as the voice in the oven's flames.

"Just as I thought. You double-crossing wretch. I brought you in off the street when you were nothing but a dirty Beach Rat." He snapped the breach closed.

"Stephen, you're not worthy of the oven's power. I will serve it the way it deserves."

Esposito raised the shotgun, aligning the barrel with Edgar's face. "Good-bye, Edgar. You're toppings like all the rest."

Edgar lunged to the side, whirled around, and hurled a knife at Esposito. The blade spun through the air with wicked accuracy. Esposito yelped as the blade pierced his shoulder, sending his aim upwards. The shotgun's blast hit the ceiling. Edgar sprang to his feet, dashed toward Esposito and flung another knife at him, but this time Esposito swung the shotgun around to bat the blade point away from his face. Edgar crashed into Esposito, shoulder first, knocking him to the floor. In the collision, he dropped the shotgun, and Edgar jumped on top of him, wielding the knife and now swiping the blade at his throat.

#

Lonnie, desperate to rescue her brother, descended the steps into the basement where the excessive heat encumbered her movements. Darkness turned to a red glow from the mouth of the great oven. At the center of the room, Edgar battled to take Esposito's life with a butcher knife.

She raised the pistol, gripped it in both shaking hands. Her brother's voice called out, *"He killed me...he's trying to kill Esposito, he will kill you next."*

Brodie wasn't anywhere in sight.

His voice seemed to be coming from the maw of the oven. *"Kill him."*

Her first shot whizzed past Edgar's ear. He scowled at her with eyes matching the fires in the forge and chucked a knife at her. She sidestepped the blade, delaying her next shot and giving him time to advance on her. At close range now, she squeezed the trigger. The bullet tore through his chin and burst out the back of his head.

He fell onto a conveyer that reached out from the mouth of the oven like a tongue. The conveyer started up and drew his body into the flames.

Esposito crawled to his feet and yanked the knife from his shoulder. "Good job...Lonnie," he said between short breaths. "Now...the gun." He held out his hand.

She hadn't realized her aim was locked on Esposito.

"Bring me back," her brother's voice

demanded.

She glanced to the oven, saw Brodie pulling himself partly out through the fiery opening. *"Help me. I'm stuck."*

"Brodie..." She fought back tears. "I don't understand," she murmured. "You should be dead."

Esposito inched toward her. "Whatever you're hearing and seeing, Lonnie, it's not real."

She snapped back to the moment and wagged the pistol at Esposito, a warning to keep his distance.

"You can bring me back, Lonnie."

"What do I do?"

"Kill Esposito. Put him in the oven."

She locked eyes with Esposito.

He recognized her look of determination. "It's not worth it. Trust me, Lonnie. I wish didn't make that deal with the demon in the flames. Profits for flesh and blood. I should have listened to the shaman."

"What shaman?"

"Ethore, the exiled Timucua shaman who'd warned Edgar and myself about the Dark Coast's sordid past."

"He's lying," Brodie shouted. *"Esposito is the devil's spawn. He's killed a lot of people for riches. He will continue to make all-meat pizzas unless you end him now. Finish it. Bring me back."*

"I have to stop you," she told Esposito. "Before more people die for your all-the-toppings pizzas."

"No." Esposito dashed at her, reaching for the gun.

She squeezed the trigger, a triple-tap. *Bang. Bang. Bang.*

He took all three rounds to the chest and fell onto the conveyer, which lumbered toward the oven's hellish mouth. Brodie's flaming arms stretched out, grabbed Esposito, and dragged him into the inferno.

Only then did she get a glimpse into

the fiery hole and saw a mass of meshed faces and limbs that swam in an ungodly sea of liquid fire. The throng of souls stretched and moaned, either welcoming Esposito or begging her not to close the oven, but Brodie was not among them. Their wails could've come straight from hell. She stepped away from their frightening screams. "Brodie? Brodie. Where are you?"

"Here," he called from behind her.

She turned to see Brodie standing near the stairs. She rushed to hug him. "It worked. Thank god. You're alive."

Brodie's embrace felt fever hot. He didn't feel like he was alive.

"It did work, right?"

Brodie showed her a reassuring grin, then he guided her to face the ominous oven. "This is our pizzeria now."

"What about your dreams of adventure...my marine biologist career? We can't give those things up to make pizzas."

"You can and you will," came a voice from the oven. *"It's the price I demand for restoring Brodie unto you."*

She gaped at the flames. "Who was that?"

"Ela, the Sun God of the Timucuans. We must serve him now, and he will require tribute, as always."

"Tribute?"

"Human sacrifices. He gets the souls, we get meat for our pizzas."

She shuddered at the thought, the savagery. "No way. I want no part of this."

"You have no choice," Ela shouted from the flames. *"Unless you'd rather take your brother's place in here with me."*

She didn't want to die so she had to concede. "Just promise me we'll serve more than all-meats pizza."

Brodie wrapped an arm around her shoulders. "Our new menu will be a big hit."

Tales from the Dark Coast

The restaurant's delivery doorbell buzzed. The siblings shared an inquisitive stare before going upstairs to investigate.

A staggering local drunk stared up at the dark *OPEN* sign.

Lonnie unlocked the door. "Sorry. We're closed."

"I'd die for a slice right now," he slurred out.

"In that case, come right in. We're under new management."

In the kitchen, the oven belched fire and smoke.

Michael J.P. Whitmer

Canvas of Shadows

Working among the open moving boxes scattered about his Ocean's Way studio apartment, Justin managed to set up his easel. Staring at the canvas, he thought about how he could fill the blank space. *Something aquatic? Beachside, coral reef, fishes and seagrass?* "Too cliché," he muttered and huffed at the idea. His internal critic had again muzzled his artistic expression. He couldn't find his muse. Moving here to the Dark Coast was supposed to inspire him to greatness. So far, only failure had followed him.

He took a pull from his cigarette, savored the fire in his lungs the watched the exhaled smoke drift out the open window. A quarter of the moon's glory hid behind streaks of high clouds in the late Florida night sky. He could hear waves breaking on the shore but he couldn't see them, as his view was of a courtyard and a span of wall constructed with coquina rock, a mineral and organic limestone abundant along the coast.

All the way down First Street stood unfinished resort buildings and high-rise apartments tarped and fenced off from the sidewalks. "Boom to bust," his Uncle Kyle had told him. Ocean's Way was the oldest Spanish architecture still standing along the coast, built of logs harvested from the swamps and imported exotic woods and erected by native Timucua slaves under the lash of European taskmasters. It had once served as a grand hotel and marina during the Roaring Twenties known as the Ruby of the Coast, and before that, a Spanish Mission and garrison, and back in time to the French conquerors. Local legends spoke of pirates, led by the Master of

Thieves, who had terrorized shipping up and down the coast and hid out in the maze of mangrove swamps that stretched upriver from the sandy shores. Today, Ocean's Way stood as a monument to a dark and deadly past, but to Justin, its ghostly mystic held in its dim glow an artist's salvation.

He blew another puff of smoke out the window and was about to turn back to his unpacking when he spotted a shadow grow across the courtyard. It stretched and shrank, backlit by a streetlamp until a black cat rounded the corner of a narrow ledge running along the exterior of the apartment building opposite his. It stopped below an open window on the third floor, and after a quick scan of the area, it leapt to the sill, fast as a blur, then disappeared behind the drapes waving in the breeze.

Justin didn't like cats. They were creepy in the way they slinked around, immune to the rules by which dogs had to abide, and they had no understanding of the English language. *Sit, stay, heel:* all Greek to them or not important enough to warrant obedience to any human. This black cat had free roam, came and went as it pleased, a carefree life of prestige and privilege, something Justin wasn't privy to but wished to attain through the mastery of a brush stroke, oil on canvas made to evoke emotion and awe for viewers far and wide.

After taking the last drag from his cigarette, he crushed it in an ashtray on the windowsill and moved back to the blank canvas. As hard as he tried, he couldn't envision an image to paint within its wooden frame. He set out his oils and palette, brushes and rags, hoping for inspiration, but none came. Even the vision of the cat's long, slanted shadow across the face of the apartment building was rejected by his internal critic. Defeated, he moved to his mattress on the floor where he laid himself down and curled into a fetal position. He had regretted staying up so late for no reward.

The next day, Justin rose early to meet Uncle Kyle out in the courtyard to help him with a sprinkler problem, as Justin had agreed to be the complex's new handyman. His uncle went on and on about a reported break-in at Ocean's Way. "A jeweled brooch heirloom was allegedly stolen. Damn snowbirds, probably lost the thing on the way down here," Kyle explained while showing Justin how to fix a broken sprinkler head.

"What did the police say?"

"Still hanging around, conducting a thorough investigation. There was no sign of forced entry. If the old couple didn't have some type of tie with a local judge, the cops wouldn't be involved as closely, if at all. Nothing else was missing. Now, Mr. and Mrs. Zokolowski are flying back to Pennsylvania, and Ocean's Way gets a black eye under *my* watch."

Tales from the Dark Coast

"That's rough, Uncle Kyle. What condo were they in?"

Kyle pointed to a third story window.

Justin felt a chill. It was the same window the black cat had entered.

#

While organizing his studio apartment, Justin only stopped for cigarette breaks at his window and to rearrange the corner of the room he had dedicated to his painting. He had stacked crates of supplies neatly on either side of the easel.

Focusing on the blank canvas again, it seemed to stare back at him, mockingly. An artist, he knew, had to be inspired, either by life's experiences or a wild imagination, both of which he lacked. Great artists found their muses in sex, violence, fear of dying, and apparitions of death. He lacked all of these motivators. This move was supposed to free up his mind, loosen his inhibitions, and kill that internal critic that always told him he wasn't good enough. That critical voice often sounded like the drunken slurs of his father, who had no problem telling him a career as an artist was worthless. He'd constantly reminded him of the high cost of the art classes Justin had flunked. Seemed scenes of flowers and cornfields hadn't inspired him to finish a single canvas.

Justin had tolerated his dad's violent outbursts, but when he destroyed an oil painting of Hades that Justin had worked on for months, he reached out to his Uncle Kyle for help, a way out, a new beginning. So far, that mocking canvas of nothingness had followed him here from New York.

He turned away from the easel, lit a cigarette, and sat in front of the open window where he could blow out the smoke. From across the courtyard, the black cat came into sight, slowly moving the length of the thin ledge on the second story of the opposite building.

Isn't that the Zokolowski's cat? Why didn't they take it with them back to Pennsylvania?

He watched it stop at an open window and wondered what that damn cat was up to. It turned and glared at him with glowing feline eyes that reflected the moonlight. Its tail flipped from side to side, and it hissed at him, showing white fangs, but Justin didn't flinch. He stared back and wondered which one of them would be the first to blink.

The cat stared.

After several moments, the eerie connection unsettled his stomach. He looked away, snuffed out his cigarette, closed the window, and shut the blinds, all the while feeling the weight of the cat's feral stare. Curiosity caused him to peek through a chink in the blinds. The cat licked its paw in victory and sprang through the open window.

A real-life cat-burglar? Justin laughed aloud at such an absurd thought.

No matter how laughable, the next day, after a sleepless night, Justin could not get the cat's stare out of his mind. The damn thing was strange, the way it stalked the night and slipped into open widows at will. He wondered whose window it jumped into last night. In the main office, he checked his uncle's records and discovered the window belonged to Henry Gregger, a retired widower and new tenant to Ocean's Way. Maybe it was his cat. Justin decided to inquire. He knocked on Mr. Gregger's door and stood silently in the hall, his heart beating wildly with curiosity. He heard stirring from within the apartment, shuffling footsteps to the door.

"Who is it?"

"Maintenance."

The locks clicked and the door cracked open. Henry Gregger, an old and gray man, looked through wire-rimmed glasses and scrutinized Justin quickly. "What do you want?"

"I'm Justin, the handyman. Kyle's nephew."

Henry's facial expression softened with the mention of the property manager's name. "I'm in the middle of something right now, sonny. Can it wait?"

"One question. Do you own a black cat?"

"A cat? I don't know anything about a cat." His voice was edged with impatience. "Do you mind if—"

"What's going on?"

"It's missing... I was wearing it before I went to bed, set it on the nightstand with my glasses, but this morning it's nowhere to be found."

"What's missing, sir?"

"An elbow macaroni bracelet my daughter made in elementary school for her mother, my late wife, Cindy. She rarely took it off."

"Oh. I'm sorry..." Justin muttered.

"I'm sure it'll turn up. Can't just walk out of here. Now I must get back to looking." He shut the door.

Justin stood there, perplexed, no longer sure his cat-burglar theory was so laughable.

#

Later that evening, Justin met with Kyle for dinner at a local eatery called *All the Toppings* that once touted the best all-meats pizza in town. The new management had opened up the menu to popular American fare, including burgers and fries. He relayed his conversation with Mr. Gregger to Uncle Kyle. "He still hasn't found it."

Kyle brushed his pile of French fries over and squeezed ketchup into the newly cleared space. "A macaroni necklace?"

"Bracelet," Justin said, stirring crumbled crackers into a bowl of chili with a spoon.

"Mr. Gregger's a nice man, but I'm not sure what we can do for him." Kyle dunked a pinch of fries into the ketchup.

"There's more. After I left Mr. Gregger's place, while I was changing the pool's filter, I overheard two women gossiping over their mimosas. One went on about how her husband couldn't find his letter-opener. Apparently, it belonged to his grandfather who served in a war."

"Does she think it's been stolen, too?"

"She didn't say that, but still, it's odd multiple tenants have things gone missing."

"People lose shit. Old people, especially."

"Maybe it's the cat."

"What cat?"

"I saw a cat go into Zokolowski's window the night their brooch went missing, and last night into Mr. Gregger's window."

Kyle looked at Justin as if he'd grown a second nose. "Ocean's Way doesn't allow pets. What are you implying, Justin? A stray cat is pilfering our tenants?"

"A stray? Sure..." He wasn't certain himself. "I don't know where the cat belongs...only that I saw the cat from my window, and it saw me. Pretty scary the way it stared at me."

"What are you doin' gawking out your window? I thought you were here to focus on your art."

"I haven't been able to sleep."

"Look, you convinced me that moving you out here is what you needed to find your muse. A clean slate is what you called it. I'm still deleting voicemails from your dad...cursing me out for taking you in. Show me you mean business. No more talk about missing old-farts' knickknacks and stray cats. You're my sister's kid. I love you like a son, and I get that your dad didn't make it easy for you to paint, but that's life.

You have passion and talent. I saw it in the art your mom used to send to me."

"I was ten." Justin forced a laugh.

Kyle chucked fries into his mouth. "Show me something you painted here."

"Easier said than done. Whatever happened to those old paintings she sent you?"

"Hell if I know. I'm old. I lose shit, too."

They laughed. Justin didn't have to force it this time.

"Finish your chili so we can get out of here. You need to get home and get a decent night's sleep."

#

That was Justin's intent when he went to sleep early that night. A rush of wind swept in through the studio window, rattling the blinds and jarring him awake. Moonlight illuminated the otherwise dark room. After crawling from bed, he set out to silence the rattling but stopped as a shadow stirred just beyond the moon's reach.

The hairs on the back of his neck prickled. "Who's there?"

"It is I, the Cat."

"A talking cat? What kind of friggin' nightmare is this?"

"Your worst nightmare." The voice was androgynous and ageless, both haunting and cold. It encircled him like the wind that swept through the window and constricted his spine in an icy vice, freezing his bones with a fear that rendered him unable to move. A talking cat was not to be trifled with...

From the shadows and into the beam of moonlight stepped the black cat, slowly but faltering, as if unsure on its own four paws.

"What's wrong with you?"

It stumbled closer and started coughing and heaving, as if its entire body needed to force something from its throat. The cat stood on its hind legs, threw its head back, and opened its mouth beyond its natural pivot until the jawbone dislocated. Its feline eyes began to swell red in their sockets, and as they were about to burst, the cat thrust forward, gagging one final time to eject a slimy mass of hair and blood that slopped on the floor in a grotesque mound.

"That's some hairball there, Cat."

The pile began to break up, revealing a jeweled brooch that shimmered in the moon's glow.

"I knew it. You're the thief."

"Now, see what's underneath." The cat laughed, still on its hind legs. Its black fur ripped off its body, and a mist of crimson revealed the feline's muscle tissues and veins, which too, shredded, leaving its skeleton and organs dancing in a puddle of its own blood.

Justin stepped back. "You've got to be

shittin' me."

The beast cackled and pranced as if performing a show in the spotlight of the moon until its body folded, bent, and imploded on itself to form a black sphere that hovered in the place where the cat had been dancing.

The sphere grew in size and began to rotate as if it were consuming the fabric of the universe to form a black hole, ever expanding and howling with fury.

Justin's blood burned with terror as the black hole began to consume him, bit by bit. He tried to scream but his head was sucked into the void, rapidly, followed by the rest of his body. An imprint of his petrified state lay trapped in thin air as if it were a miniature event horizon where nothing could escape. The look of horror on his face could have been painted on canvas by the Devil himself.

A hammering knock at Justin's apartment door sat him upright in bed. His hands flew to his face, felt his head, his neck, his chest... All there... "What the hell?" He looked to his window and blinds, they were closed. His eyes darted to the spot where he had seen the cat's horrid ballet. The bloody hairball and brooch were gone. There was no sign the strange scene was anything more than a nightmare.

The knocking continued, frantic and insistent.

He rolled from the mattress and stagger-stepped to the door. Through the peep-hole, he made out Kyle's face and two other blurred bodies bunched behind him in the hall. Opening the door, Justin let his uncle in. "What time is it?" He rubbed sleep from his eyes.

Two policemen entered with him, and Kyle's face registered a seriousness Justin had never seen before. "What's going on?"

"Justin, these officers suspect that you may have stolen the missing jewelry."

"Yeah, right. Me? A thief?"

"I tried explaining how absurd that is, but they have a warrant to search your premises."

"Okay? I don't have much."

Justin's cooperation didn't seem to change his uncle's bothered expression, making Justin anxious as the two officers looked around the apartment.

"What the hell are you looking for?" Justin asked.

"Keep calm," Uncle Kyle said in a hushed tone. "The Zokolowskis must have pulled some strings to get that damn warrant."

"What probable cause could they have?"

"These guys have been questioning residents for the last couple of days. It was brought up how you'd moved in the night the brooch went missing."

"I hadn't even finished unpacking... like I had time to..."

The officers seemed to have found

something by the easel.

"What's that?"

One officer, followed by the other, approached with a paint rag in his white gloved hand. The unraveled cloth revealed Zokolowski's jeweled-brooch. "How do you explain this?" the officer demanded.

"I-I don't understand," Justin muttered. "I've never seen that brooch before." *Except...in the nightmare...*

#

The cops escorted Justin downstairs and out of the courtyard. Kyle followed until his nephew was placed in the back of the police car.

"It was the cat, Uncle Kyle." Justin cried. "That damn cat planted it—"

The car door closed and shut him up.

Kyle couldn't respond to such a farfetched notion. "I know, buddy," he muttered. "I know."

Out of the corner of his eye, where the

coquina wall turned behind the building, the black cat sat staring, waiting, its tail flip-flopping.

Kyle stalked toward it, mad enough to choke the little shit.

Alluringly, the cat moved along the wall until it ducked out of sight behind the building.

Picking up his pace, Kyle rounded the corner, but the cat was nowhere in sight. "What have you done?"

The moonlight shrank and the cat's shadow grew, stretching from the wall to the building and cloaking Kyle in an unnatural darkness.

"I righted your blunder with the brooch," an ancient voice screeched from the gloom. "The local authorities have been meddling about. You underestimated the Zokolowski family's connections."

"Why involve my nephew?"

"He sought me out, just as you did. Now his destiny is mine."

"Forgive me for disagreeing, master...but I don't want him to end up like me. Justin has aspirations. He'll be a great painter one day."

"He doesn't have what it takes. Besides, you have no say in the matter...or have you forgotten your place?"

Kyle was suddenly entrapped in a whirlwind of shadow pressing in on him from all sides. He had little choice but to concede. "Of course, master." He began to inch back toward the courtyard. "He is yours."

The darkness retreated, and the light of a new day broke through. The cat's cloak of shadows lifted. Kyle trembled the entire way back to his office, kept his feelings under control and avoided curious tenants. "Why were the cops here?" "Was it your nephew who done the stealing?" "I never liked that guy." "He's not a real artist." "When's the trial?"

\#

The jailer awoke Justin and patted him on the back. "Come on, pal. You're free to go."

He rose from the cot, seemingly in slow motion, and squinted under the bright ceiling bulb. The cell smelled of roses and chocolate instead of the usual vomit and urine. Odd, he thought. Surreal.

The jailer showed him through several checkpoints, one where he had to sign his name and collect his belongings. Suddenly, he was standing outside the jailhouse, bewildered. He pulled out a cigarette, lit it with his Zippo, and put the lighter back into his pocket. Blowing smoke, he muttered, "Now don't this beat all."

Spent and still feeling imprisoned, Justin set off walking toward Ocean's Way. He strode down First Street, past the dunes where a boardwalk, bustling with artists and browsers, led to a pavilion stage set up on the beach for nighttime concerts. At the Aqua Lounge, he only broke stride to sidestep a small line of people waiting to get in. Music and revelry emanated from within, but as tempting as it sounded to join in, he was in no mood to party and kept walking. Before long, he trekked across the parking lot for Masque Media, a Dark Coast tabloid, and a used furniture store. A boarded-up public library stood across the street, basking in the shade of palm trees. He passed the skeletal frames of buildings under construction, long abandoned and overtaken by windblown sand. The feeling of death and decay created a macabre veil that seemed to blanket the beaches.

He soon found himself looking up the face of the coquina wall that surrounded Ocean's Way. It wasn't hard to imagine Spanish conquistadors pacing the rim and guarding the broad entryway. Today, however, instead of soldiers, the black cat sat atop the wall and glared down at him as if he were the enemy.

Damn cat.

He felt suddenly dizzy, disoriented, and before he could question why or how, he was reaching for the doorknob to his studio apartment. Now he stood before his easel, the canvas no longer blank. He studied the impressionist image of himself, his eyes wide with fear, and his mouth open as if screaming in terror. He felt like he was looking in a mirror, but he had no memory of painting it, though his hands were slick with fresh paint. In the fresco's background, he'd included his mattress where the black cat sat, its glowing red eyes boring into him, tail in mid-swipe. Gripped with horror, he tore the painting from the easel, tossed it to the floor, and stomped on it until the paints were all smeared together like a Crayola box meltdown.

I couldn't have painted that. Even if I possessed the muse to create such a masterpiece, I would never have destroyed it. The *cat must be screwing with my head.*

Suddenly, everything went black. The sound of his heart beating out of control echoed in the darkness. Stumbling, he tripped over his mattress and landed across the bedsheets, gasping for air, flailing and kicking until panic choked him to unconsciousness.

He awoke to see distorted steel bars; he was back in the jailhouse, lying on the cot, and encompassed by an unholy aura. As he sat up, he saw his uncle sitting on the edge of his own cot in the adjoining cell. Metal bars separated them. "Uncle Kyle?"

He didn't respond, just sat there, petting the black cat in his lap, stroking its fur with gentle, loving caresses.

Hot rage flooded through Justin. "You traitor. You knew it was the cat all along." He leaped through the bars as though they were but a mirage, lunged at Kyle, and wrapped his hands around his throat.

"Justin, what are you doing?"

The cat screeched, leapt to the floor and arched its back, its hackles standing on end. *"Kill him, Justin, and take his place at my side."*

He realized the cat was directing Justin's hands to squeeze the life from his uncle. "No. Stop."

Kyle tried to scream but only struggled for air.

The cat directed Justin to wrap his uncle's neck with a bed-sheet and finish the act of strangling him to death. *"Court trails can get messy. Suicide is more fitting."* The cat chuckled.

"Uncle Kyle, I'm sorry. I can't stop."

Kyle reached out to give him a folded letter, his last act of life.

Justin took the letter, but before he could read it, his body expanded and then disbursed to dust that now funneled through a vortex of darkness. Instantly, he stood in Kyle's office at Ocean's Way, his body cloaked in an ominous dark haze.

The bookcase at the far wall slid aside, revealing a hidden passage. Shadows directed him through the opening where he descended stone steps beneath the complex. A rock slab rolled away, revealing a chamber reverberating with sounds of the sea. He found his corporeal body lying in a collapsed heap at the entrance.

Justin blinked. He looked up from the cold wet surface of the grand cavern's entranceway. The strange sheet of darkness had lifted, and he felt intact once again. Torches burning ethereal flames illuminated ancient carvings on the walls that intrigued him to inspect further. Containing his fear, he followed the corridor into the cave, hoping for a closer view of the walls and the stalagmite in the center.

Behind him, the stone slab rolled shut, but he couldn't take his eyes from the faded reliefs of fear-stricken faces chiseled in stone. One portrait after another gazed at him with their petrified expressions. Thousands of faces adorned the chamber's encircling walls. He found an engraving of Uncle Kyle glaring at him with the same horrified expression as when he had taken his last breath. Adjacent to his uncle's image, Justin's terrified portrait stared down at him, the same horrific image he'd seen painted on the canvas in his room.

The cat's looming shadow slinked across the limestone wall. This was its lair, he finally realized. The anger he had bottled up, unleashed all at once, flooding his bloodstream with hot adrenaline, but some unknown force froze him in place.

What had first appeared to be a large stalagmite turned out to be a mountain of loot piled up in the center of the chamber. Countless oddities and relics: some gold, jeweled, and shimmering, and others less luxurious like the macaroni bracelet he spotted at the foot of the structure near a stack of his childhood paintings rolled up like ancient scrolls. All the items had a sentimental feel but were splotched by a dark growth that seemed to be consuming the lot. At the top of the giant stack, a black hole rotated cosmically, a phenomenon he'd seen before, in his bedroom, at the beginning of this nightmare.

The black cat's feral laugh resonated throughout the cavern.

But this was no nightmare. His instincts screamed at him to retreat the way he came, but he couldn't move, as if his spirit had been entrapped.

"You reek of fear. Good. Like your uncle and those throughout eons past, you will serve me." The cat's voice thundered around him, crippling him further.

He fell to one knee, bowed his head and was about to utter the words *I'm yours, master…* But stopped. Justin remembered the letter from Uncle Kyle, now wadded in his hand and damp with sweat. He quickly unraveled it...three words:

Burn it down.

His spirit fought back. He remembered the lighter in his pocket, scooped up his childhood paintings, and put them to the Zippo's flame. They caught fire, and he set them around the base of the mountain of loot. The flames took hold of the dark growth, flammable as sawdust, which climbed the pile at a rapid rate until the fire reached the cosmic, swirling black hole.

Justin ran for the corridor, blocked by the huge stone, fully intent on rolling it aside, when shadows stretched from all sides and grabbed his limbs and throat, stopping him cold.

The cat's voice boomed furiously. "What have you done?"

The fire eating away at the stolen treasure caused the cat's shadow-grips to loosen, as if the loot gave the cat its power over humans and dominion over the Dark Coast. As the lair filled with flames, Justin broke free. He rushed to the stone slab and rolled it aside then dashed down the corridor to the stairs. With smoke and flames at his heels he entered Kyle's office. Fire alarms sounded throughout Ocean's Way. He didn't look back as he ran out to the hallway and joined the flow of tenants exiting their apartments. They hustled out of the building and scattered about the courtyard, but when a portion of the second and third floors collapsed onto the first floor, they realized they were too close to the inferno and scrambled past the coquina wall to gather together on Third Street. The flames were shooting a hundred feet into the air.

"Good God," someone shouted from the crowd.

The Ocean's Way residents had all made it to safety and watched heir belongings go up in smoke. The fire department arrived en masse, and it took them thirty minutes to stop the inferno from claiming both buildings.

Justin found Mr. Gregger and stood beside him, watching the chaos. "I think this is yours." He held out his hand and opened his palm where the macaroni bracelet lay.

The old man's face lit up with pure joy. Before he could ask where Justin had found it, a firefighter rushed out the coquina wall entranceway. "I've got a survivor here. Found it under some rumble." He was cradling the black cat in his arms.

It meowed and looked right at Justin. He expected its shadow claws to lash out and impale his neck to choke him in full view of the witnesses from Ocean's Way as they danced around his suffocating body. However, no display of such power occurred. Instead, the cat squirmed free from the fireman's arms and scurried to Justin's feet where it flopped down, rolled over, and exposed its pooch to be petted.

Uncle Kyle walked up, looked down at the cat, and then frowned at Justin. "Is this the black cat?"

"Yes, but it's different..."

"Don't look scary to me."

"You've never seen this cat before?"

"Not that I can recall."

Justin knelt to the cat and rubbed its tummy. If Uncle Kyle knew the cat, he'd obviously forgotten it and the evil hold it had on him and Ocean's Way.

The cat purred under Justin's gentle touch.

He suddenly envisioned his art set up on the boardwalk and passersby stopping to admire his work and inquire about prices for the many finished canvases displayed about. He faced the ocean, a brush in hand, his paints, easel, and canvas now under his full command. The black cat sat on a railing post, posing, completely inert in front of a sunrise, the colors bursting across the sky and down the shoreline.

Across the street, his studio was open for business. *Canvas of Shadows Gallery and Gift Shop.* There on exhibit hung his greatest work of art: *1,000 Faces of Fear,* a montage of the many wide eyes, gaping mouths, and locked expressions of horror he'd recreated in oils from the reliefs he'd seen etched in stone in the cat's lair, now a burned out cavern beneath Ocean's Way.

The moment he stopped petting the cat, the visions of his future dissipated like windblown sand. He scooped up the cat and embraced the rush of creativity filling the empty canvas that was his imagination, now plush with fresh ideas.

He gave the cat a gentle squeeze. "I finally found my muse," he whispered in its ear.

"Meow."

The Curse of Dark Pointe Shores

On the southern banks of the Dark Coast lay the pristine beaches of Dark Pointe Shores where its landmark Lamp lighthouse still stands on the eastern-most jut of sand and limestone to warn ships of yore to steer for deeper waters. It was built atop an old Spanish garrison that once housed conquistadors whose galleons stood sentry over the inlet bay to the Matanzas River. Today, its arc light was dark atop the faded red-and-white tower, and the sturdy stone building beneath it housed, not soldiers, but marine biologists of the Dark Pointe Marine Institute. As with most stretches along the Dark Coast, history had marred Dark Pointe with bloody invasions, wars, and

Timucuan slave uprisings. Most recently, though, a new mystery surrounded Dark Pointe. Women were disappearing.

Instead of cannon-laden galleons, the bay teemed with shrimpers, those squatty trawlers with towering outriggers from which hung webs of netting and the hopes of many a shrimp fisherman. One of those hardy men of the sea was Captain Christopher Jones. He, with his hardy wife Margret, set sail, as they did every morning in their shrimper, *The Joneses.* Dawn had yet to break, but its glow was already snuffing out starlight over the horizon.

From his chair in the wheelhouse, he motored out to trawl the Atlantic shelf for those succulent pink-fleshed delicacies. It was mid April, the heart of the shrimping season, and he expected a grand haul. Margret stood aft on the trawl deck, looking out across the water toward the sunrise, her face to the breeze, and her red hair a firestorm in her wake. She loved setting sail, those first few minutes riding the chop to open water, the smell of brine, and the freedom of the sea.

He made a turn south, set the diesel to trolling speed, and left the wheelhouse to operate the winches. Margret stood starboard, manning the net lines as the outriggers lowered until they were nearly horizontal with the water. Captain Jones worked the port lines, feeding out slack until the floaters hit the rushing water and opened the mouth of the nets. Margret gave him the thumbs up, so he rushed back to the winches and trawled out the nets until the spool hubs were exposed. He pulled the spool lock levers for the two-hour trawl, one hour south, turn around, then one hour north.

"Settin' pretty," he muttered and returned to the wheelhouse where Margret had poured two mugs of steaming coffee from the thermos.

"It's a beautiful morning." She offered

her mug in salute.

He tapped his mug to hers. "For a beautiful woman."

She smiled and sipped coffee.

Though she wore a heavy green seaman's jacket with the collar upturned and thigh-high rubber boots over her jeans, she was his idea of the perfect runway model. He'd leave the bikinis to the college girls who visited the shores for spring breaks and summer vacations. Margret was the girl for him, always was, always would be. Someday they would have children, settle down in some landlocked town, but not today, not tomorrow, but someday.

He set the mug on the sideboard and went to work checking the GPS, rudder trim, and the engine RPM. Over the course of the trawl, he expected the bow to nose-up and the RPM to decrease as the nets became heavier with harvested shrimp. If one net held more bounty than the other, the shrimper would tend to turn in that direction, so he'd use the GPS to steer a straight course. A hundred yards out to port, the lights of other shrimp boats trawled along, and as the sun finally broke the horizon, he could see an armada of boats stretched out fore and aft for miles and miles.

"Steady as she goes, Captain." She gave him one of those two-fingered scout salutes. "I'll go out on deck to check the lines." She ducked out of the hatch.

Twenty minutes into the trawl, Captain Jones boosted the RPM and trimmed the bow down. Visions of fat nets and big checks played in his mind. Smiling, he stood and peered out the aft window to see Margret had removed her heavy jacket and boots, as the Florida sunshine heated the air quickly. Now she looked rough-and-tumble in a red sleeveless pullover, jeans, and white deck shoes. *Best lookin' first mate in the fleet.* Off the starboard gunwale stood the old lighthouse, as majestic as ever.

An experienced seaman knew when something was going wrong. The lug of the diesel, the tilt of the bow, ever so slightly it grabbed his attention, and even before the starboard outrigger bowed and cracked, the swing of the stern threw him off-balance.

He heard Margret scream in surprise, saw her topple over, but he didn't rush to her aid. Rule number one of the sea: never stop steering the boat. He jerked around in his chair to see the wheel spinning to starboard. Grabbing it, he stopped the spin but the shrimper suddenly listed right, a near forty-five degree bank. His coffee mug went flying. The GPS showed a hard right turn. The RPMs dropped to near dead-engine.

Throttle up. He gave her the gun and steered hard left, hoping to right the ship. His first thought was that the starboard net had snagged on the bottom, a rock outcropping not on any maps...or worse, he'd netted a whale, an impossible feat for such a small net. Still, the boat wouldn't right itself and started taking on water over the stern wall. He had to get off the throttle, release the wheel, and hope the boat would stay afloat long enough for him to drop the starboard net.

Fighting the slanted deck that would spill him into the sea, he clung to rigging and storm rails all the way to the winches. Margret was already there, pulling on the winch lock levers, but they wouldn't budge. He lent a hand, and between the two of them, the starboard lock let go. The net lines spun from the spool so fast they sang and snapped through the pulleys until the outrigger broke free and plunged into the depths. The boat bobbed upright and wobbled on its keel.

"What the hell was that?" she shouted.

"The end of the trawl, for us." He wiped sweat from his forehead with the sleeve of his jacket. "Let's get the port net up, see what we can salvage."

She unlocked the spool, and he engaged the winch. The lines started to spool in. She ran to port to tighten the outrigger lines that counterbalanced the weight of the net. Every part of this job she knew like the back of her hand. He couldn't have been prouder—

The winch suddenly stopped and the net line snapped like it was but a thread in grandma's sewing kit. As the broken line whipped through the pulleys, he shouted to Margret, "Look out."

She jumped back just as the line shot past her and ripped down the outrigger, snapping like a bullwhip. The net broke free, and the boat rocked on its keel to starboard. Captain Jones held on to the winch lever for dear life as gravity and inertia tried to rip him from the deck. It didn't get much worse than this for a shrimper.

However, as the boat bobbed upright, the gates of hell opened to prove him wrong. Seawater surged over the port gunwale, pushed upward by some subsurface force he'd never seen before. And from the bubbles and swells rose the bluish translucent tentacles of some ungodly creature. First one, then two, then three tendrils writhed in the air, each tipped with a barb like the stinger of a jellyfish. At first the tendrils waggled and whipped about without purpose, breaking the outrigger supports like they were toothpicks and busting out windows on the wheelhouse.

Captain Jones became a prisoner of his own fear, frozen in one place, unable to scream, unable to breathe, but mostly unable to believe his eyes.

Lying flat on her back on the deck, Margret screamed. The sound attracted the tentacles, and they swooped over her, hovered for a moment as if assessing the situation, then they arched their barbs downward to impale her body and raise her off the deck, kicking and screaming, her red hair flailing in the sunshine.

"No," Captain Jones shouted, now believing his eyes, and with no concern for his own safety, he grabbed a fire-axe from the wall brackets and rushed toward the beast, hoping to sever its tendrils and return his love to him, but he was too late getting to the deck, now slippery with a translucent slime that dripped from the wrecked rigging. The bluish arms of death retreated into the roiling sea, taking Margret with them, never to be seen again.

He screamed.

Then the nightmares and drinking began.

Captain Jones was never the same man after he lost Margret. He never again went shrimping. At low tide, *The Joneses* leaned in the sand, only to float when the tide was high, but always anchored in the bay. He'd barely possessed the strength or will to repair the outriggers and replace the nets, but he did, and out of respect for Margret's love of *The Joneses*, he kept her fueled and seaworthy.

Up-beach from the shore, he'd opened a little bait shop in a shack he'd built and painted blue and white with little starfish decals scattered about. Nemo swam beneath the only window. The porch was adorned with life-saver rings, fish nets, seashells, and every other thing nautical. A single white rocker stood to the left of the front door where he'd sit and watch the world go by, him and his best friend, Jack Daniels. He slept in a room in the back; a simple cot, mini fridge, and a Bunsen Burner on the counter were all he needed for furnishings. It was a simple life for a lonely man with a broken heart.

Most nights he drank himself to sleep, dreamed of a beautiful redhead, bright sunrises, and blue-limbed monsters rising from the sea. Night terrors, he'd called them...when he'd wake up screaming. Some nights were worse than others, but nights like tonight frightened him the most, nights when he heard his name whispered on the wind.

"*Christopher...*"

He stirred from a drunken stupor, eyes wide open, ears tuned to the sea. Waves rolled to shore, the ocean spray hissed, and he heard it again.

"*Christopher...*"

Dressed in only his boxers emblazoned with seahorses, he rose from his backroom cot, stumbled through the bait shop, and made it outside to the porch. "Margret, where are you?"

In the distance off the coast, a storm brewed up a display of lightning flashes, the thunder far from the reach of his ears. He saw the silhouette of the old Lamp lighthouse backlit by the storm, and the windows glowed in the Marine Institute at its base. *The Joneses* floated on its keel, the gentle waves slapping against the hull. It was high tide. But no Margret.

"The sea's still got her, as always," he mumbled.

He sat in the white rocker and looked out into the night, the bay so smooth, the sea so calm under the moonlight. But something was out there, a translucent nightmarish beast, something not known to any man or of this world, he had begun to believe.

"Christopher..."

At the foot of his chair where he'd left it, the bottle of Jack rested, nearly empty. He picked it up and swigged what remained, hoping the booze would silence the calling. However, the voice on the wind persisted, as a siren would call a sailor to his death, pulling at his heart strings, reminding him of what he'd lost to the sea.

"Christopher..."

He had to go, he had to know if she

would be free of the sea monster this time, the desperate hope of a broken man. He rose from the chair as if his mind and body were controlled by forces beyond his comprehension. He needed to sober up, sleep it off, but he'd leave that for tomorrow. Tonight he had to know...

He stepped down the porch steps and set off across the sand to the shoreline and turned left to go farther down the beach. His feet sunk in the sand but he trudged onward. He was a man with a purpose, as his name on the wind ushered him toward a splintered jetty. It was once a boardwalk pier, vibrant with life, music, food, and fanfare, now left in ruins in the wake of a hurricane, which one he couldn't recall. There had been so many—

"Christopher..."

Approaching the canted and broken wooden beams that once supported the pier, he saw movement among them, a woman with red hair that flowed like liquid fire, dancing in an elfin way, barefoot on tippy-toes and twirling without a care.

Margret, is that you? The words formed as a thought and never left his lips.

His legs found the strength to run, fueled by thoughts of a lost love found. He kicked up sand, racing toward his beloved. When he arrived between the pillars, she was gone. A mirage she was, a trick of lights and shadows, all combined to drive him mad.

"Margret," he yelled and dropped to his knees in the sand. "Why do you torture me so?"

A wave broke and slipped to shore, bringing with it his lost love, Margret's skin aglow in the moonlight, her hair like fire in the breeze. He was speechless as she glided toward him, her arms outstretched, but her eyes were fixed and glossed over.

He whispered, "If this is a dream, please don't wake me up."

In silence, as always, she pulled him to the sand where the waves met the shore and embraced him in arms as cold as the sea. Their lips met, hers fishy to the taste, and then she straddled him, had her way with him, more forcefully than before, as if every movement was made in desperation to achieve the final high. He felt used, in a way, dirty, but if this was the only way to keep her in his life, he'd take it, as frightening as it was, the way she didn't gasp for breath, or moan, or cry out at the end.

As they lay together in the splash of the surf, he saw something about her he hadn't noticed at first. Her belly was round and the skin undulated with writhing life from within. He sat up in shock, his heart beating like mad. Could these late-night liaisons have produced a child? Could she be carrying his son, his daughter? "You're pregnant?"

She rose to her bare feet and pointed

out across the bay to the Lamp lighthouse and the lit windows beneath the dark tower.

"The father? He's there?" Or the monster that took her? What was the connection? What evil lurked at the Marine Institute? "Talk to me, Margret. What's going on?"

The night came alive with the siren's song, so sweet, so serene, so alluring. She took his hand and led him into the breakers.

He pulled back, let go of her hand. "No. I won't go with you."

And she was gone.

He staggered backward to the safety of the shore, fighting for breath as if he were drowning, and stared at the swells rising and falling. "Where did you go?"

Again, she appeared, this time carrying a bundle cradled in her arms, and now she was smiling, her eyes bright and full of joy.

"What is that?"

She brought it to him, an infant swaddled in kelp leaves, an odd looking fellow, bell-shaped head, and eyes that did not blink, just stared at him. His little hands had webbed fingers and tiny claws. Three gill slits gasped on each side of its neck.

He jumped back. "Where did you get this...this..?"

She pointed toward the Lamp lighthouse.

He knew she couldn't have gone that far to fetch this wretched creature. The sea monster, it had to be the monsters' offspring. "The bay. The father's in the bay?" What devil's work was at hand—?

She shook her head no and pointed right at him.

"Me?"

She nodded and parted the kelp to show him it was a boy.

"My god. I'm his father?"

She hummed a siren's high note.

He pointed to her round belly. "Who is the father?"

She slipped back into the sea.

"The monster's? Tell me who."

Only the whispering wind held the answer, but silent as it was now left him stunned inside. He trudged back to his shack, back to his cot, and cried. Tomorrow would be another day to mourn, to miss his Margret, miss his son, and drink himself into another stupor.

#

As it happened every year, Dark Pointe Shores was a popular *Spring Break* destination. College students from all around the South descended on the beaches, partied in the streets, and generally put the locals on edge. Sex, booze, and rock-n-roll rambled in on buses from as far north as Virginia and as far west as Texas. One particular party bus would fall prey to the Curse of Dark Pointe

Shores. Some of these students would never make it home.

Evelyn Baker was one of them. She had to get away from Tybee Island, Georgia, and a boyfriend who was as clingy as Velcro. And there was Chad Davis, a real piece of work when it came to the ladies. If ever there was a match made in heaven, this wasn't it.

Saturday night, while the bond fires blazed on the beach and teenagers drank until they puked, Evelyn strode down-shore with her camera strapped around her neck. There was so much beauty here to behold and memorialize. She focused on the waxing moon, near full in the sky over Dark Pointe. Its radiance illuminated an old lighthouse, the upraised shrimp boat outriggers in the harbor, and an array of wooden struts jutting from the sand. She snapped pictures with her Nikon SLR on automatic flash, determined to capture the mood of her first foray into freedom from

Sam. Poor Sam. Sam. Sammy. They had a good run while it lasted, but like most young love, it went the way of the Dodo Bird.

"Hey, there you are."

Oh, crap. Not Chad again.

She snapped another shot of the moon. Chad may have been a funny guy at first, but now he was an annoyance much worse than a stone in her shoe. He couldn't take a hint. They were road-trip buddies on Spring Break, she'd told him, not spit-swapping coeds. "Why aren't you at the party, Chad?"

"I lost you back on the dunes." He jogged up to her, looped an arm around her waist, and leaned in for a smooch.

She managed to face-palm his lips and jerk away. "What's wrong with you, man?"

"Come on, girl. I thought we were cool." He threw his hands up and plastered a pout on his lips.

"You may be cool. I'm not. I just got

away from an idiot boyfriend. I don't need another one. Besides, this trip for me is about seeing the sights and breathing fresh air." She held up her camera and snapped a shot of his whipped puppy-dog expression, the flash washing his face in white. "You're mucking up my photo shoot, man."

"Ah...you aren't that cute, anyway." He whirled around and slogged off through the sand toward his drunk friends.

She had to shake her head. *I'm cuter than he deserves.* Still, she knew she'd see him again when they got on the bus to head back home. She snapped a picture of the lighthouse. If she could climb to the top, she'd be like Rapunzel, locked in a tower where no one could find her.

Not even Sammy.

Everything she didn't want in a man, Sam had it, but rather than bail on him, she had 'settled' all throughout high school. It seemed he was the best guy her small island town had to offer. When she was accepted to Georgia Tech, she thought that would put a gentle end to their relationship, but guess who showed up at her dorm room door. If that wasn't a shocker enough, he bent the knee and presented her with his grandmother's wedding band. "Will you marry me?"

She hated him for that, for making her put her foot down and tell him no. Yeah. She'd broken his heart, but his obsession for her was borderline psycho.

She turned her camera to one of the jagged pillars jutting up from the sand. There, bright moonlight illuminated the weathered wood where the dead hulks of crustaceans clung...and something else, carved initials: M+M, encircled by a heart cut deep. She wondered who they were, if their love had lasted the test of time, or had it ended up on the scrap heap of broken promises and dashed dreams. She snapped a flash picture, and in search of more lovers' graffiti, she strode barefoot into the surf to inspect the other canted columns. Those she found, she photographed and came to realize this pier, in its better days, was a beachcomber's lovers' lane for hooking up.

A sudden jolt of cold shudders skittered up her body, as if she'd just stepped into the Arctic Sea. The ocean surged and came at her, a stupendous wave that bubbled with white water aglow in the moonlight. She turned around and ran, but something grabbed hold of her ankles and dragged her down. Rolling on her back, and her camera flashing pictures on rapid-fire, she saw in the strobing light, blue tentacles rising under the moon's glow, then barbed tips slammed into her chest with such force the wind got knocked from her lungs. She hadn't the breath to scream for help or cry out to God.

Paralyzed by fear or venom, she didn't know which, she was powerless to fight back as the tentacles constricted around her body and dragged her under the surf and into sudden darkness.

#

And then there was Chad, good-old-boy Chad, smitten and bitten, and he didn't take rejection lightly. Fuming, he'd made it far enough down the beach that he could hear music and laughter coming from the party he'd left, hoping to make a score on Evelyn. And what a score that would have been, a roll in the sand and surf under a moon so bright. Spring Breakers would forever remember his name and his conquest—

He stopped when he came upon four women, seemingly from out of nowhere, completely nude, their skin glistening in the moonlight as they splashed in the surf, like pixies, innocent and giggling. They all stopped at once and waved for him to come join them.

He rubbed his eyes, thinking he was dreaming. What kind of heaven was Dark Pointe Shores? Shot down by one and beckoned by four... "Hell yeah." He forgot about Evelyn and rushed headlong into his best fantasy ever.

They remained silent, swooned and swarmed around him.

"You gals must be locals." Chad couldn't get out of his clothes fast enough. Each young nymph took turns kissing his neck, his chest, and farther down, passing him around as they circled him like—

Pain shot up through his abdomen and crashed behind his eyeballs. He was dragged under the water, into the deep where filtered moonlight reflected off a school of fish swimming toward him...wait, not fish but needle-toothed eels with webbed hands and tentacles, no, not eels, but some kind of sea creatures that attacked him with teeth and claws.

#

On the other side of the sand dune that separated the beach from the access road, a charter bus idled in a sand-swept parking lot. Its lights were on, and its driver was impatient to get on the road. He had to take this busload of drunk and rowdy college teens back to Georgia, but his headcount was short by two idiots.

A frat boy in a torn wife-beater T and piss-stained shorts leaned over the back of the driver's seat. "Give him five more minutes, pops." He'd probably puked himself sober enough to carry on a rational conversation. The others back there were either passed out in the seats, necking, or by the smell of it, puking their way back to sobriety. "It's not like Chad to be late like this."

"I've waited long enough."

"His dad will kill him if he misses this bus."

"And the girl? What's her dad gonna do?"

"Evelyn? She's an air-head, man, on the run from Tybee Island. I bet she'll keep going to Key West and Cuba."

The bus driver grumped. "Every trip there's always some love birds who wander off on their own."

"Not Chad and Evelyn. No way."

"I have a schedule to keep." He put the transmission in gear.

"Five more minutes, pop."

"You want to go ask the locals if they'd seen them?" The driver gestured across the parking lot to a group of fisherman types, milling around a sheriff's car, probably gathering to enforce the 2am beach curfew. "Go ahead, but you'll probably end up in jail. We should have been out of here twenty minutes ago."

It was no secret that the locals of Dark Pointe had no love for the townies coming in to raise hell and party on their beaches, and they had no qualms against administering vigilante justice.

"I think we should hit Daytona Beach next year." The frat boy walked back down the aisle and sat with his luggage.

Diesel engine rattling, the bus lumbered onto the access road under the sheriff's narrow-eyed glare.

#

A few days later, another stranger arrived in Dark Pointe Shores, driving a Cadillac SUV and wearing shades like Joe Cool. He checked into a fleabag motel called *The Gypsy*, just off the main highway. The lobby was congested with folks checking in, checking out, or just hanging around.

"Welcome to Dark Pointe, young feller." The manager handed him a cardkey for Room 112. "Honeymoon suite. I expect you won't be staying long."

"Long enough to find my girlfriend."

He held up a photo for the man to inspect. "Have you seen her?"

He frowned, didn't even look. "Sonny..." he checked the sign-in log, "ah... Mister Jenkins—"

"Sam. You can call me Sam."

"Bit of advice, Sam. People in these parts don't take to strangers askin' questions. You look a might road worn—"

"I drove straight through from Tybee Island, Georgia."

"How about you get some rest, clean up, get yourself some food over at Mary Cracken's Diner, and come see me in the morning? We'll talk then. As you can see, I'm a tad busy right now."

The manager was right. A hot shower and a quick meal put him right to sleep. He dreamed of Evelyn, the love of his life...but what's this? She's in the arms of another man. And who was this redhead calling his name? He awoke with a start, heart beating like mad. The morning sun splayed out around the closed curtains. Breathing heavily, he stared up at the moldy ceiling and struggled to calm down.

His head was filled with fragments of the dream. One reality was for sure. He'd lost control of his life, gone bonkers when the chartered bus pulled into the Tybee Island station and Evelyn didn't come down the steps. He'd hoped she'd blown off some steam, got her head on straight, and was ready to again run to his waiting arms. His fondest memories of her drove him on a mission to set the world right, take his woman back home, and live happily ever after. Some might say he was delusional, but true love would not be denied.

Showered and dressed in Bermuda shorts and a Hawaiian-style shirt, and wearing leather sandals, Sam crossed the sandy parking lot shared by the Gypsy Motel and Mary Cracken's diner. He noticed his bug-splattered Cadillac needed a good washing, and he wondered if there was a carwash somewhere down the road of wood-framed buildings and homes, most built on stilts to stand above the high water of storm surges that might breach the dunes. This stretch of road was called Oldport, creased between the Atlantic and the swamps of the Dark Coast wetlands. From here he could see the lighthouse tower and the up-rigging of ships in the harbor. Maybe Evelyn had decided to settle here, find a place, get a job, and invite him to join her later. Least she could have done was told him of her plan so he wouldn't be worried to death.

The motel's OPEN sign flashed red and blue neon. Inside, the manager scowled as if displeased to see Sam had returned with his questions. "Good morning, sir." His forced hospitality was evident in his flat tone of voice. He stood behind the lobby counter. "How did you sleep?"

"Not well, honestly, but not the room's

fault, though."

The manager nodded. "Thanks."

"You told me you'd answer some questions—"

"No. I told you strangers with questions are frowned upon in these parts."

"Yeah, that too. Like I was saying yesterday, I'm looking for my girlfriend. She came into town on a bus about a week ago."

"You mean a party bus? Yeah. Spring Break. I remember a lot of them buses packed with townies who made drunken revelry down at the beach. Far as I know, they all left the day after, before the sheriff was gonna run 'em off."

"Do you remember this brunette with curly hair?" He showed him the picture of Evelyn taken in a photo booth at the Georgia County Fair.

"No..." The manager squinted at the photo. "There were lots of pretty girls, but can't say I remember any one of 'em. Your girlfriend, you say? What she doin' on a party bus and boozin' on the beach?"

"We've had our problems, but I know she loves me."

"Good for you, but them gals got some of the locals in a fuss."

"How so?"

"I bought this motel a few years back, moved up from the Florida Keys, so I don't know all there is to know about Dark Pointe Shores, but the area has a history of women gone missing, and any women passing through are unwelcome by the locals."

"Women around here go missing? Like kidnapped?"

"Look, I'm not the one to be asking. It's local talk. You want the whole story, go ask around at Larry's Fuel Depot. The shrimp fishermen gather there..."

#

Tales from the Dark Coast

In the gravel parking lot of Larry's Fuel Depot, two trucks with boat trailers hitched to their bumpers were parked in front of an old wooden building the size of a warehouse. Sam parked his Cadillac between the trucks and walked inside. The place smelled like dirty socks. Rows of shelves held everything from chips and candy to boat parts and tires.

He followed the signs to the Anchor Bar and pushed past the double doors leading into a dark corridor. At the opposite end, a red neon sign flashed PUB above the entryway. Though the sun was uncontested in the midday sky, the saloon was barely lit. Hanging fans creaked from the vaulted ceiling where open gable shutters let in light and the birds. Seagull shit littered the weathered rafters.

Now ain't this quaint?

At the bar, three male patrons sat atop stools and nursed from their bottles of beer. The barkeeper, a large burly man, hairy but for his head, stood behind the bar, polishing a glass.

Sam took a stool closest to the bartender. "Hey, how goes it?"

Two locals who smelled like fish glanced at him with no respect and no reply.

"What can I do for you, boy?" The bartender spoke with a cigarette hanging from his lips.

"A drink. How about a—"

"We don't serve your kind in here," he growled. "Damn townie."

Sam peered at the other patrons, noticed their faces turn mean, lips curled, eyes narrowed. A cockroach in their midst would seem more welcome.

"How about some information, then?"

The bartender slammed the glass on the counter. "We got no information either."

Undeterred, Sam pulled the photo from his pocket and held it up for the barkeeper to see. "I'm looking for this girl. She was here a week ago...on a party bus passing through."

The brute glimpsed at the picture and then shared a look of disdain with the others at the bar. "She's just another damn townie."

They shifted on their stools as if they were about to pounce. The nearest guy broke the neck from his beer bottle and waved the jagged edges at Sam.

Fighting panic, he scowled. "Hey. I don't want no trouble."

The bartender produced a pump Remington from behind the bar and jacked a shell into the chamber. "Well now. Guess you got more trouble than you bargained for, boy."

"Oh shit." Sam abandoned the barstool and held up his hands. "Come on, man. Don't shoot."

From the far end of the bar, a wild-eyed man sprang from his stool and rushed at Sam. He had a leather-tough appearance only gained from excessive labor under the sun. His calloused hands grabbed Sam by the collar, forcing him in reverse toward the exit. "Get outta here, grommet," the old sailor yelled, spurring the other patrons to laugh.

"What's the matter with you people?"

Outside in the gravel lot, the man unhanded him. "We don't take to townies askin' questions around here," he hissed. "Now git movin' before ya git killed."

"You saved my life. Who are you?"

"Don't matter none...look...ya probably deserve the truth. You want it, come find me south of the old pier. I have a bait shack on the beach. Be discreet, grommet. They're watching you."

"They? They who?"

"You don't learn too quick. Stop askin' questions around here."

#

Captain Christopher Jones sat in a white rocking chair on the porch of a blue and white shack, facing the waves rolling in from the bay. The water shimmered under the midday sun, where *The Joneses* bobbed on its anchor. It was high tide. All around him, fishing poles, nets, and seashells of all sizes and shapes were on display for customers, should any dare approach the drunken proprietor. He spotted Sam trekking up the beach toward the bait shop and stood to stare him down with his wild-eyed look.

"Hey," Sam said as he approached the porch.

"I figured ya wouldn't show, grommet," the Captain said in a voice cracked with age and worry. He held a half-empty bottle of Jack Daniels in his fist.

Sam raised his Joe-Cool shades to set them atop his head. "My name's Samuel."

"They call me Captain Jones." He swigged from the bottle and stroked his gray beard.

Sam stepped to the porch rail, smelled the alcohol on the captain's breath, and offered him the photo. "Sir, I'm looking for my girlfriend. Her name's Evelyn. Have you seen her? Any information will help."

Captain Jones's gaze hardened. He made a noise somewhere between a laugh and a grumble before snatching the picture, and turning away from Sam, he shuffled back to his chair where he studied the girl's image, curly hair and perfect teeth. It was easy to imagine Sam and Evelyn together, two young lovers pressed cheek to cheek and smiling. "Another one," he mumbled.

Sam climbed the three steps onto the cluttered porch and stood next to a pirate's chest, closed to protect the gold within, he mused. "Another one, what?"

"Foolish love." Jones swigged whiskey and offered the bottle to Sam.

"No, thanks."

He shrugged and returned the photo to Sam. "You be better off leaving Dark Pointe while ya can...only more heartbreak waiting for ya here."

"So you know where she is?"

"Women missin'...ain't really missin' in Dark Pointe. What the sea takes, she'll never return."

Sam wasn't sure what to think about the jumble of words he was hearing.

"We all gotta pay," Jones went on. "Some more than others, but once ya go, there ain't no comin' back. She'll have you in the deep."

"Who? Evelyn?"

"She belongs to the sea. We got no choice but to accept our fate. Others know that, but be damned if they can do nothin' about it. The rest might try, but end up takin' their pleasures in hell." Captain Jones stood from his chair and staggered to the pirate's chest.

Sam stepped aside to watch him open

the lid.

"You havin' dreams, too?" Captain Jones stared into the open chest. "We all git 'em. All who lost her. It's her way of talkin' to us, saying she's ready. It's the memories that make us want, the love that links us...allows her control when she's callin'."

The mention of dreams triggered the recall of Sam's own nightmare, his beloved with another man, a redhead with his name in her whisper, causing his heart to beat fast and his palms to sweat. He wanted to leave, to hear no more of this nonsense about she and the sea, but Captain Jones was bent over the chest, blocking the porch steps.

He removed a green seaman's jacket and held it to his heart, lovingly as an infant child. "I couldn't save her."

Damned if there wasn't a tear in his eye.

"I should be going, Captain Jones. I think you need to be alone." Sam tried to squeeze by him.

The captain turned around, nearing uncomfortably close, and pressed his bony finger to his own wrinkled and tanned temple. "It's in here, boy, every time I held her hand, shared a smile, it's there for her to lure me back. My Margret will forever be in my dreams, as with you and Evelyn. All she need do is say your name, and she'll have you if ya ain't careful."

Samuel glanced down into the open chest, saw a fair woman's photograph in a polished frame, her hair as fiery red as a sunrise, a striking resemblance to the redhead of his dream, the stranger whispering his name. Smiling next to her stood a younger Captain Jones. There was no doubt she was the loss he had endured, the pain that drove him to the bottle, the fate that caused him to talk in circles. Sam realized the captain couldn't help him find Evelyn. "Sorry about wasting your time, sir."

"You have what ya need, grommet. Don't be fooled by what ya hear on the wind. Don't answer the call. Just run, my boy, run."

"I'll remember that." He pushed past Captain Jones and hurried back up the beach toward the Gypsy Motel, and with his shades back in place, he blocked out any notion of Evelyn being forever lost.

#

That night, asleep in the motel, he dreamed dreams that tormented him. He should have felt safe and warm and loved, strolling the beach with Evelyn under the light of a full moon, but she was uneasy, full of angst he couldn't understand.

"I feel trapped," she muttered.

Waves broke around them, but his eyes were locked on hers. "Trapped? How?"

"It's this place...this nowhere town. Tybee Island is suffocating me. I have to go."

"But you said we'd be together forever."

The surf rushed over their bare feet.

"What we had...we lost, though you may wish otherwise." She touched his bare chest. Her hand felt colder than the mist rolling in off the ocean. He reached out, grabbed her around the waist, and drew her into him. Their paired shadows stretched across the sand under the leering glow of the moon.

"Please...stay. I love you."

"Goodbye, Sammy."

He felt her body slip from his embrace. Her flesh beaded into water droplets and streamed into the surf where she broke like a wave and joined the tide that carried her out to sea.

"Evelyn, come back." He chased after her, each step slogging in soft sand that sucked the power from his legs. In slow motion, he ran to catch the retreating shoreline, never gaining ground, losing her more and more with each second...

Sam shot upright in bed, his breathing heavy like he was still battling the sand. "Evelyn. I'm sorry. I can't find you."

"Sammy..."

He blinked...listened.

"Sammy..." Her voice was calling to him from the sea.

"Evelyn?"

"I'm here, waiting for you."

"I'm coming." Enchanted and filled with hope, he threw on his shirt from yesterday, climbed into his shorts, and ran from the motel in his bare feet. He rushed across the highway toward the shoreline but encountered a row of rolling dunes that blocked him from his beloved.

"Sammy..." came to him on the wind.

Ignoring the warning signs: KEEP OFF DUNES, Sam tackled the incline, and once over the top, he stumbled down to the shore where he trekked in a daze, throwing glances behind him, expecting Evelyn's footsteps to be there, but it was only the surf he heard, surging up the shoreline and washing away his footprints.

"Sammy..."

His name seemed to fly on the wind that carried him to a ruined jetty, a skeleton of a pier that jutted up from the sand in splintered pillars, a monument to disasters past and memories lost. Coupled initials enclosed in hearts were engraved in the weathering posts. He wished S+E had a heart among them.

"Evelyn. I'm here. Where are you?"

A wave crashed on the beach, and Evelyn emerged from the swells as the water rolled in. Her body was nude, her skin paler than the moonlight that reflected off the sand. She glowed divine as she approached between the leaning pillars of ocean-rotted wood. *"Sammy..."* Her siren-sweet voice sang in his mind, though her lips didn't move.

Rooted in the sand, he couldn't believe

his eyes, but he wanted to believe with every fiber of his being; he wanted her back again, like the way they were before she left Tybee Island. "Evelyn."

She appeared to glide toward him without leaving a single footprint. Her skin turned translucent and iridescent, as if absorbing the moonlight itself, but her stringy hair seemed coated in slimy gelatin. Beauty, mystery, and danger stood before him, but the sight of her flooded his mind with memories of their most cherished moments: their first date, their first kiss, their first dance... An underlying fear gushed over him. He remembered Captain Jones telling him to run, but foolish love stayed his feet from flight.

She pressed her full cold lips to his, and though they felt slick and smelled fishy, he kissed her deeply and swore he'd never again let her go.

Slyly, she pulled him to the sand and caressed him into a frenzy. He felt immobilized by the mixture of mystery and passion that surged through him.

Finally back in her arms, "I love you," he whispered.

As the waves retreated, Evelyn mounted him.

#

He'd barely noticed the moon's sweep across the sky until it was directly overhead. The sand glittered, the wave crests glistened, and Evelyn's gooey hair clung to his face. They'd made love like two hungry animals, she on top, in complete control, but she never said a word. He trembled as they lay together on the shore. "Are you okay?"

She moaned.

"Evelyn, say something."

He shifted his weight under her and saw, protruding from her back, a translucent blue tentacle that reached up into the moonlight and then arched down into the surf. A sudden terror tied knots in his stomach. Something evil had a hold on her. He grabbed the appendage and yanked on it, hoping to remove it, but Evelyn's body was jerked off of him and hauled back toward the sea.

Sam scrambled after her and threw his arms around her waist. "You're not leaving me. I love you. You love me. You're mine, so stop before I do something we'll both regret."

Dragged into the ocean with her, he held his breath as they were yanked past the waves and pulled into the depths.

Before him, just where the moon's reach from the ocean's surface began to fade to the shadowy deep, he beheld a sight more terrifying than the revelation of losing Evelyn again, a great creature in the form of a jellyfish floating in the murky abyss. From beneath its giant, gelatinous umbrella-shaped bell, hundreds of blue tendrils writhed, some with a female corpse impaled on the barbed stinger. Among the dangling women, some of their stomachs were round and squirmed with unseen life.

His lungs burning and begging for a breath, he released Evelyn's waist to swim for the surface, but froze when he saw the woman with sunrise red hair, the same fair woman in the photo with Captain Jones, safeguarded in his locker of lost memories. Her face was creased with pain as she hung from a tentacle, her belly round. A woman's body dangling beside her disgorged dozens of small creatures that swam in circles then darted toward him.

The spawns' hydrostatic skeletons were formed from a mass of translucent jelly-like matter: bluish, glossy, and slippery skinned. They swam using squid-like tentacles that protruded from their backs and paddled with webbed hands and feet. Their heads were bell-shaped with mouths lined with needlelike teeth and eyes incapable of blinking.

He looked to Evelyn. She stared at him blankly, as if she couldn't care less about the predicament he was in. He kicked for the surface, but the swimming spawn attacked him, latching their teeth into his skin, and he felt the sting of injected venom. Tentacles held onto him tightly as his nervous system shut down and his muscles locked, and as body sank and his last breath bubbled from his lungs, he heard the whisper of Evelyn's voice in his mind:

"Sammy... I don't love you anymore."

#

The night wasn't going much better for Captain Jones. He tossed and turned on his cot behind the bait shop, his mind maddened by shrieks of terror coming from the sea.

"Christopher..."

Three translucent blue tentacles rose

up around his cot and whipped about his tiny room, knocking the coffee pot off the Bunsen Burner. It was only a dream, a nightmare he tried to escape, as he did every night, only to awaken with those screaming night terrors.

"Christopher..."

He sat up on the cot, trembling, glanced around his tiny place, the single nightlight illuminating the coffee pot spilled on the floor, the Bunsen Burner tipped over. The nightmare had come home to roost...or had he, in last night's drunken stupor, upended things..?

"Christopher..."

"Oh, no, Margret. Not now."

"Come quickly...it's Sam...I'll show you the way."

"Sam? Ya know Sam?"

"I know you keep The Joneses *fueled, batteries charged. There's not a moment to spare."*

He stood, scratched his beard, and

suddenly realized she was speaking to him, telepathically from the sea, and not as usual in his slumber. She never spoke, so something desperate had her in a tizzy. Fighting to clear the Jack Daniel's fog in his head, he turned on the ceiling light, a single naked bulb that revealed a translucent bluish slime dripping from his cot, his counter, and the floor was slippery with the goo. He blinked and the slime was gone, but this vision he could not ignore.

It only took him a few minutes to throw on his seaman's clothes and climb the rope ladder up to *The Joneses'* deck. He cast off the anchor line, fired up the diesel engine, and motored into the bay, his heart raging with the dread of going back to sea where monsters snatched loved ones from the decks like candy from a dish.

Setting sail at night was dangerous, and he was thankful for the light of the moon to keep him from crashing into the shore as he motored out of the bay, his rigging lights aglow. In the wheelhouse, he didn't have to steer, as the wheel was turning this way and that of its own accord. He felt Margret's presence in the chair, he didn't know how, but he knew what she told him to do.

"The winch, the portside net, take her down."

#

Sam felt his body being pulled upward. He was going to heaven, he thought, but the pain remained, and his mind still rang with Evelyn's goodbye, which stung worse than the hell spawn feeding on his flesh.

As long as he felt pain, he knew his body was holding on to the last thread of life. It felt like more of an out-of-body experience than true consciousness when he realized he'd been scooped up in a net and dragged off the seabed, along with those bloodsuckers. He heard the lug of a diesel engine, the creak and moan of winches and net lines, and the splashing of water as he broke the surface.

The winch whined as the outrigger rose and swiveled the net over the trawl deck, and he heard the whoosh as the bounty was released and scattered on the deck, his limp body along with the flopping fishes, pink shrimp, and ravenous creatures. His out-of-body vision turned to black.

The next thing he knew, he was coughing up salt water as Captain Jones hammered his chest with CPR. Sam gasped and coughed and wished he were dead, as the creatures reminded him that he was no longer at the top of the food chain.

"Damn fool," Jones shouted. "I told ya to run. Now look at the mess you're in."

Sam could only cough, his vision bleary, no doubt from the creatures' venom.

Captain Jones peeled a handful of

squirming suckers from Sam's arm, only to be bitten by the gnarly bastards. Something evil had invaded Dark Pointe Shores, and he had an inkling it might be the spawn of the sea monster that had taken his Margret. Who would know for sure? He looked out to the Lamp lighthouse tower and the lit windows beneath it. The Marine Institute. They would know.

"You hang in there, grommet. I'm gonna get ya some help." He ran to the wheelhouse and set course for the lighthouse dock.

Sam lost consciousness.

Getting closer to shore, Captain Jones motored *The Joneses* through a semicircle of buoys with *NO WAKE* emblazoned in red on white. At the end of the dock, a sign read: *Property of Dark Pointe Marine Institute. Authorized Personnel Only.*

He had no sooner tied up to the dock when a contingency of technicians spilled from the old stone building. They wore white hazmat suits, rubber gloves, and protective face shields and goggles.

"He needs help," Jones told them. "Some kinda mutant life-form...they're eating him alive."

None of them said a word, just climbed aboard, and scrambled over the deck, picking up the creatures as fast as they could. Another team wheeled out a glass tank filled with water, into which the creatures were placed, now swimming about like freshly hatched fry.

"Do you all know what them things are?"

"Top secret," a man said, his hands full of squigglers.

Dumbstruck, Captain Jones watched them work around Sam's body but paying him no mind. "What 'bout him? He needs medical attention."

"He's as good as dead," a gruff voice came from behind him.

Jones turned to see a man standing on

the dock, a head taller than the crew of technicians. He wore a scarf around his neck, neatly tucked into his suit coat, and he sported Theodore Roosevelt's spectacles. "Do something, for Christ's sake."

A harried technician approached the newcomer. "Dr. Hyde. Some of them are already dying. We're going to get them into the hyperbolic chamber immediately."

"Very well. I will meet you down there." He turned to one of the aides. "Martin, get a gurney out here." He indicated the man lying on the deck. "Let's get him inside, as well."

"Yes, sir."

The others wheeled the water tank down the dock and into the building.

"What are them things that damn near ate him up?"

"I think you know. Margret is pregnant, and not by you this time."

"The sea monster's spawn. I knew

it...but how the hell do ya know about Margret?"

"I know everything about her and what took her from this very deck. Frightening, I'm sure it was."

"Nobody believed me 'bout the monster, not the sheriff, not the Coast Guard..."

"I did."

The technicians loaded Sam onto a gurney and carted him off the boat.

"Is he gonna make it, doc?"

"Is he a friend of yours?"

"I saved his life...twice. How do ya know 'bout my wife? What are you people doing here? What secrets ya keepin'?"

"You have many questions. You may come in with him."

Inside, they wheeled Sam into a lab, complete with bubbling beakers, glass tubes routed every which way, and what looked like a coroner's autopsy table, stainless steel with a water faucet and hose.

A tinge of formaldehyde spoiled the air. Captain Jones watched from a window as the techs laid Sam on the table.

The aide who went by the name Martin stood next to Dr. Hyde. "Well done, doctor. A specimen like him will serve our facility immensely."

They looked down at Sam.

He moaned, barely conscious. In his mind, an echo of regret found purchase. *I should not have followed Evelyn to Dark Pointe Shores.*

"A fine mess indeed." The doctor prodded Sam's body with his gloved hands. Chunks were missing, and the parts that remained were swollen with poison. "Administer the serum."

Martin took off his gloves to fill and operate the syringe, a seemingly impossible task with his webbed fingers and long claws.

Captain Jones stood there speechless and remembered his web-fingered son.

Could Martin be one of Margret's offspring as well?

#

Sam awoke on a moving gurney but couldn't find the strength to lift his head and glance around. The pain in his right leg made him wish he was dead. He would have screamed but his mouth was gagged. It seemed as if he had only one eye, as the other wouldn't open and felt like it was taped shut. A creature must've made mincemeat out of it.

His hands and arms were wrapped in white bandages and strapped to the gurney as if he were a wild ape that might do someone harm. He looked up and noticed that the man pushing the gurney had webbed fingers with long claws, and there were three parallel slits in his neck that looked like fish gills. That hallucination he chalked up to the venom coursing through his veins.

Captain Jones walked next to him, a welcomed sight. The last thing he'd heard him say was he was going to get him some help. At this point, this so-called help wasn't encouraging.

He noticed he was being wheeled through an old stone building's hallway. Some doors were to classrooms, some to labs, and some were closed and made of riveted steel. Whatever was shut inside those rooms, the Marine Institute didn't want to get out. The gurney stopped at a door that opened automatically. The sign on the wall read: Faculty Only.

Inside, a tall man stepped up to the gurney. "Good to see you're awake, Samuel Jenkins. We thought we'd lost you there for a while. Martin, these straps won't be necessary. Sam's not going anywhere." He patted Sam's shoulder. "Ain't that right, buddy?"

Sam tried to say, "I'm not your buddy," but he could only mumble, what with the gag and all.

As Martin released the straps, Captain Jones stepped back, and the tall guy introduced himself. "I'm Dr. Hyde, at your service. I had my staff bring you to me once you regained consciousness. You've been out for five days. Yes, my boy, you've suffered a great ordeal."

Sam tried to say, "I'm not your boy, either," but again only mumbled. He raised his freed arms to see they looked like giant Q-tips, his hands balled in bandages.

"What the hell?" only came out as incoherent grunts.

"Sorry about your mouth being bandaged. We had to remove your tongue."

At that, he tried to scream, but with the same muted result. *Why had they cut off my tongue? Are they afraid I'd seen the monster and its captive women, and I might tell the authorities?*

"So our conversation might seem a bit

one-sided. As the sedative wears off, you'll notice, more and more, the necessary measures we had to take to preserve your life. It was unfortunate that your obsession with Evelyn, your constant stalking of her, has brought you to this situation. You should have let her go and moved on with your life. Instead, you crossed paths with *C-yudosi-Numa.*"

"Cum-o-huh-a?" he muttered.

Captain Jones frowned. "What is C-yudosi-Numa?"

"Have a look on the desk."

There he observed an old leather-bound tome, the title in French, he believed, by Theodore de Bry, and stacks of notes... A drawing caught his eye: Timucuan natives gathered to watch a giant jellyfish, its tentacles drawn as rays of sunshine, fall from the heavens. "What is this?" he asked the doctor.

Hyde joined him at the desk. "The Fish God from the Sky, a Timucuan deity worshipped by the Cult of C-yudosi-Numa. It's the image Jacques le Moyne discovered in a limestone cave and relayed to Theodore de Bry. The original painting was destroyed when the Spanish invaded Dark Pointe and ousted the French." He lifted the heavy tome. "Published in Frankfurt, 1591, le Moyne's significant account of his transatlantic voyage with Jean Ribault's expedition to the new world. In it he writes extensively about the cult and the virgin sacrifices made to C-yudosi-Numa."

Captain Jones scowled. "You saying this is the monster what took my Margret?"

"When women of Dark Pointe began to go missing, and the extensive searches turned up nothing on land, we here at the Marine Institute thought the bodies must be in the water, so we dispatched ships with sonar and submersibles to scour the bay and the shrimp fishing lanes. There we found our kidnapping culprit, all right, C-yudosi-Numa. Seems the shrimpers had awakened it from the deep, and it came here to breed."

"Breed our women?" Jones shouted. "It must be hunted and killed—"

"On the contrary, good captain. It's a god, not a freak of nature, not a werewolf or vampire, but a fascinating study for the future of mankind. We've really come a long way."

"Are ya nuts?"

The doctor moved to a wall and switched on a light that illuminated recessed glass cylinders all in a row, each with a creature in one stage of development to another, floating in fluid. "The preserved bodies of C-yudosi-Numa's offspring," Hyde said with a whisper of awe in his voice. "Babies, toddlers, teens. You see, its genome is far more superior to our own, but ocean's conditions for reproduction polyps are primitive to it. My science isn't an exact science, more a series of minuscule discoveries that led me to a biological breakthrough when I altered its DNA so it could produce viable offspring with the women it had captured."

Jones grumped. "How...why?"

"I gave it some of my DNA." He indicated the percolating beakers on the counter. "In the process, I nabbed some of C-yudosi-Numa's DNA. The women impaled on its tentacles became pregnant, and genetics found a way to preserve the human race."

Sam threw a fit that didn't amount to much of a distraction, just mumbling and throaty groans, but in his one white-rimmed eye, Jones saw sheer terror.

"He saw somethin', didn't he. Something more horrific than the swarm of creatures what attacked him. Didn't he?"

Dr. Hyde removed the scarf, rather theatrically, to reveal slits on each side of his neck that appeared to be gasping like a fish out of water. "Like I said, we've come a long way."

Jones stared at the anomaly, his heart slamming in his chest. "What have ya done?"

Martin stepped beside the doctor, proud as any boy could be, his gills, too, on full display. "I was born this way, a cross between human DNA and C-yudosi-Numa's."

"His life started as a hostile and very hungry tadpole type, like those offspring who attacked you, and over the years, he matured into what we have here. However, as you can see..." He motioned to the floating dead creatures. "Most of his siblings didn't make it past adolescence. However, I was able to use their blood to create a serum that can change people into aquatic humans." He tipped his head to Sam. "Ain't that right, sport?"

"Sport?" Sam shouted with as much

hate as he could muster, which could have been "I love you" the way it came out, muffled and all.

"See for yourselves." Hyde opened a panel on the wall that revealed a thick glass window with a view into the ocean. There in the milky depths floated C-yudosi-Numa, the Fish God from the Sky, its mighty dome undulating just beneath the surface, and its hundreds of stringy tentacles wavering in the current. It swam toward the window as if attracted by the light inside the room.

"We call him Father," Hyde said with a proud smile.

Captain Jones stepped to the window, and there, within perfect view dangled Margret, a rag doll it seemed, her red hair floating around her head, her eyes blank and staring. The writhing within her big belly was the only sign of life. To see what had become of her, the dire situation that was her fate, spurred within Captain Jones an anger that brewed murderous intent. He turned on the doctor, fists and teeth clenched. "It's your fault my wife is dead. It's your monster."

"Monster? No. It's a god. And she's not dead, just different."

"Then I want my wife back."

"That's not within my power. Father is keeping her alive. It impregnated her, yes, and all the other women gone missing on Dark Pointe Shores, and for that purpose Father keeps them alive. Isn't it enough that C-yudosi-Numa lets you visit her in the night, make love with her when she's ready? It's not over until it's over, captain, so be thankful it's not over yet."

Jones stared deadpan at the sea monster. "She belongs to the sea," he muttered.

Hyde turned to Sam. "But you, no sir, Evelyn didn't love you, but she still went to see you, on Father's mercy, but you ended up here because you couldn't let her go. At least Captain Jones had the sense to not follow Margret into the sea."

In the window, Father raised the captive women to the glass, one at a time, as if showing off its prized possessions.

"She showed me my son," Jones said. "Is it really possible I have a son?"

"If she said so. A mother would know. And it is possible. Father has the ability to use your DNA, same as it did mine, to produce an offspring with both males' DNA, if it wants."

Jones's face turned red as if he were mad enough to pop. "I want to see him. Where is my son?"

Dr. Hyde stepped up beside Jones and pointed out the window. "He's out there, swimming freely in the deep, waiting to mature and walk upright on land...like Martin here."

"Are there others?"

"Maybe. I don't know, but it doesn't matter."

Tales from the Dark Coast

"Will he ever come home?"

"The sea *is* his home, as it was yours, Captain Jones, though I see you have forgotten."

Father swung Margret up to the glass again. If she saw the captain, she didn't show recognition in her eyes, just that cold blank stare, face-to-face as they were.

"Close it," Jones demanded, sank to the floor, and wept.

Dr. Hyde closed the panel. "You may think my experiments are barbaric, dastardly, or downright cruel, but I've a reason for doing them." He turned off the siblings' lighted cylinders. "Amphibians. Aqua-humanoids. Call us what you like, but we are the future of mankind. It won't be long before the earth's air is so foul it'll be toxic to human life, everyone choked out by CO2 and methane gas. From the sea, man emerged, and to the sea, man will return."

He walked back to the gurney.

"Consider yourself a pioneer, Sam Jenkins, a human who can truly swim with the fishes."

Sam wanted to scream but didn't even try. He'd bet money his neck was bandaged up to his own gills, as well. He had to get out of here. His flight instinct kicked in. He sat up on the gurney, spun his legs over the edge, and jumped, only realizing too late that his right leg had been amputated at the knee. His momentum threw him to the floor, yet he still tried to crawl to the exit, knowing full well he'd never make it.

"Patience, my boy. Why so hasty? Our experiments on you have only just begun." The doctor shed his lab coat like old skin, and squid-like tentacles reached out from his back and snatched up Sam from the floor. "And there's a little venom in my bite, as well. Do you want a demonstration?"

Frantically, Sam shook his head no, but

Dr. Hyde would not be denied. His mouth opened wide, revealing a barbed stinger for a tongue, which lashed out, pierced Sam's chest, and injected a surge of hot venom into his body. A sudden pain in his head felt like his brain was about to catch fire, and then the lights went out.

When he came to, he found himself in a stone room with a riveted steel door. The air smelled damp, mossy, and he heard the gurgle of water. His bandages had been removed, and he gaped at his webbed fingers and long claws. He didn't need a mirror to know he had gasping slits in his neck. His amputated leg had grown a fin. He couldn't stand, but he could crawl, which he did, and splashed into a pool that turned out to be quite deep as he swam to the bottom where he settled and breathed.

He wondered what they were going to feed him.

#

On the beach, rocking in his white rocker on the blue and white bait shop's porch, Captain Jones was having another long discussion with his best friend, Jack Daniels. They talked about the romance of the sea, monsters, and a son he'd never know but always love. They'd never play. ball, never go camping, none of it, but still, he was a father in his own right.

The Joneses still leaned in the sand at low tide, and maybe one day he'd take her out again, but not today, and most likely not tomorrow. From it all, he'd learned that obsession with a woman could take a man down a dark path. Sam Jenkins had learned the hard way. Jones had visited him in his fish-pond prison, talked to him some about his situation, his captors, now like family to Captain Jones. Their conversations were a bit one-sided since he couldn't talk. Officially Sam Jenkins was missing and presumed dead, but dead or not, he'd been living in a hell of his own making, anyway, wanting a woman he couldn't have. Same as Captain Jones over the loss of his Margret. Now he knew she was alive, though be it in her own private hell, but they could still spend time together on those warm Dark Pointe nights, find a tiny bit of happiness under the moonlight, and they would take that over nothing, any day.

Yeah. Life was good selling worms, and lures, and fishing poles, and hanging with his buddy Jack Daniels while he waited with great joy and anticipation for those nights when Margret would whisper his name on the wind. She was his gift from *C-yudosi-Numa* for however long their lives would last.

Michael J.P. Whitmer

Epilogue

And there be told the Tales from the Dark Coast, but a more dangerous, more evil, and more destructive force is about to invade the warm Florida beaches. A storm is coming, and she has a name: Guabancex, Goddess of the Wind, Mother of Storms, the Destroyer of Everything. Only one force stands between Her and the total annihilation of the city, and that would be The Guild of the Beach Rats, in paperback and e-book from TWB Press.

About the Author

Michael J.P. Whitmer is a dad, husband, and speculative fiction and horror writer living in his sunny hometown of Jacksonville Beach, FL. He won the Watty Awards Best in Horror 2010 for his story "Day of the Undead Sophomores" and 2016 Theme of Absence's Halloween Horror Fiction contest for "The Girl in the Window." His other fiction has been released throughout the web and can be found in print anthologies UnCommon Lands, See Through My Eyes, and First Came Fear. His "Guild of the Beach Rats" is another Dark Coast inspired tome.

Michael J.P. Whitmer

**Enjoy more short stories and novels by
many talented authors at**

www.twbpress.com

**Science Fiction, Supernatural, Horror, Thrillers,
Romance, and more**

www.ingramcontent.com/pod-product-compliance
Lightning Source LLC
Chambersburg PA
CBHW060747180626
46818CB00002B/479